Xalata Orbit and M
The Hammer of As

CW01481503

A novel for teenagers of every age.

By

Nick Evans

To Nathan
With big snogs !
Love
Nick

Copyright notice

Xalata Orbit and Melody Fret - The Hammer of Asttar

By

Nick Evans

Published by Nick Evans Publishing

BH1 2LH

First published, 2015

Updated February, 2016

Second update, February 2019

© 2019 Nick Evans

Dedicated to Gabrielle Hadley, my soul mate

A silent traveller

It was about half a kilometre across by a kilometre long and it rotated along its length in a lazy motion that belied its purpose. It had sat in the outer reaches of the Asteroid Belt, between the orbits of Mars and Jupiter, since the solar system had formed and the leavings of the planet-making had simply gathered together to form a band of left-over rock and minerals that rarely moved ... unless they were pushed.

This nameless rock had been pushed, quite deliberately. Engineers had captured it, built massive nuclear fusion devices on it to give it a thrust out of the belt and had detonated the devices to send the asteroid on a new path, towards the terraforming fields on Mars, building a habitable planet out of a hostile environment.

It rushed silently through space, its presence unnoticed by anyone other than those who sent it. Its final objective was to hurtle through the atmosphere of Mars and impact the surface of the Red Planet at high speed, throwing up rock and minerals, spilling out its own ammonia-rich core, helping to kick-start the greening of the planet and the creation of a breathable atmosphere.

But then, something changed.

Chapter One

The moment she was grabbed, Xalata had kicked with both feet, as hard as she could. The satisfying "Oomph!" that exploded from her attacker, when she made contact with her foot, was soon followed by her being wrestled out of the darkness through a door into a much lighter area. She shouted for help, but a gloved hand was quickly wrapped around her mouth so that she could barely breathe, let alone scream.

"You've caused quite enough trouble," said a rough voice, "and we need to keep you quiet. We don't want to wake the bogeyman do we? Now, are you going to be a good girl and make no noise, or shall we gag you? I have a lovely dirty rag here to stuff in your mouth," and the speaker waved in front of her face a piece of oily cloth that looked as if it had been used for cleaning drains. Xalata nodded to show that she agreed to be quiet, although every part of her was straining with the impulse to scream.

She couldn't see her attackers as they held her from behind, but the sound of their voices was slightly muffled, as if they were wearing something over their faces. She felt a bag being pulled over her head and the last thing she saw was a view of a very derelict-looking area of habitat that had no place being part of the Outpost.

Another voice laughed and Xalata was hauled onto some sort of vehicle where she was dumped like so much luggage. Her hands were tied behind her back and her feet were fastened together with strong, thin bands. Then the hands let go of her and she was left lying on her front while the two attackers evidently climbed into seats on the vehicle and drove her silently away - to where, she had no idea.

As she lay there, she felt her hands going numb from the tightness of the bands and so she tested them but they were fastened firmly and, as she wriggled, they cut into her wrists and ankles, making her gasp with pain. Then she tried to move her head to see if she could manage to find a chink of light to see out from under the hood. Nothing. So she stopped moving and listened carefully. The vehicle hissed along on near-silent wheels, making little jolts as it passed over slight unevenness in the tunnel through which they were driving. The two kidnappers - for such they were, she realised in horror - were not talking, keeping silent because perhaps they did not want to give away any more than they had already. She had not recognized the voices, but she was in no doubt that she would know at least the one voice again, if she heard it.

The vehicle travelled on and the silence simply grew deeper. So, what had she seen when she was attacked? The light had been bright in the space she had entered, but the area looked totally unlike the rest of the habitat that made up LunarBase. In fact, it looked more like the images she had seen on the newsfeed about the attack on Habitat 14. As she considered what she had actually seen, she recalled a large space with blast-damaged walls and smoke patches as well as broken furniture and fittings that were strewn around. But was she remembering the newsfeed or was it what she had actually seen? She couldn't be sure as her mind was in a whirl from the adrenalin pumping around her body.

Still the vehicle zipped along and Xalata had a strong sense of motion whenever it went around corners - but that happened very rarely. The gentle hum made her feel quite sleepy and, despite being very uncomfortable, she fell into a sort of shocked sleep where wild dreams screamed around in her head.

*   *   *   *   *

She couldn't tell how much time had passed when she felt the deceleration of the vehicle and heard sounds of a much larger space, voices echoing and the noise of heavy machinery. The motion stopped altogether and she felt the two attackers get down from their seats and muffled talk that she could not make out. All at once, rough hands picked her up bodily and carried her away from the vehicle.

"Where am I being taken?" she shouted. The answer was a quick thump on her shoulder.

"Be quiet," the same rough voice again. "We don't want to hear from you at all. I still have the gag so just behave. You, my dear, are just a pawn in our little game."

The other man laughed again, but said nothing. She heard the hiss of an airlock door being opened and she was put down on the ground. Someone cut the binding on her feet and she was dragged upright again.

"Right, now, you walk. No silly tricks - just behave like a nice girl, my dear, and nothing'll happen to you." With that, one of the men pushed her forward, still with the bag on her head and she stumbled to stay upright as the sensation began to return to her numbed feet and, without any vision, her balance was unsteady.

She staggered along the corridor, guided by a firm hand on her shoulder and lurched through another airlock into a space where there was very little sound. They all stopped and Xalata was pushed down onto a seat and someone undid the ties on her hands.

"Don't make a move until we leave. If you decide to take a peek at who we are, that'll be the last peek you make, my dear." *Again with the 'my dear' bit*, thought Xalata.

"You can't get out of this room. Food will be brought to you and you'll have everything you need. Your job is to sit and wait." With that, she heard footsteps retreating and the airlock door closing. There was a clunk as it resealed and then everything was silent.

She paused, listened again and then decided it was safe to remove the bag on her head. *Rename myself, Edna Bagg,* she thought and laughed, despite feeling very scared. As the bag came off she looked around. There wasn't much to see. She was in a standard type of lunar habitat living space. It was small, with a table and chairs, a couple of armchairs, a large screen on the wall and a kitchen area with a cooler. Everything was a neutral grey colour and there was no decoration or ornamentation at all. *To be honest,* she thought, *this could be my home.* But she quickly discovered that it wasn't.

She got up and wandered around to explore the space - first trying the airlock door to see if it would open. Nope - no luck there. Not that she had really expected that people would go to the trouble of capturing her and then leave her in an unlocked room.

In the kitchen space the cutlery was all flimsy plastic - no weapons there then. The cooler contained some drinks and a couple of parcels of ready to cook food: all standard stuff. Through a door to the left of the kitchen was access to a shower room and then a single bedroom with a bed made up. There were clothes in the wardrobe - her size and style: *Someone was expecting me,* she thought.

So why had they captured her? What was the plan? How was she a "pawn" in their "little game"? She thought suddenly about her dad and what he would think when he found she had been captured - *if only I had been able to tell him where I was going. And Glitch isn't going to tell - he's in on it!* With sharp realization, she suddenly recalled that her friend - so called - had betrayed her, right there in the Outpost. Why? There were plenty of questions - no answers.

Chapter Two

Previously

"For Frank's sake!" muttered Xalata Orbit as she stepped out of the immigration area and, through the group of travellers exiting the immigration lounge, saw the leering face of Adolf Fark set eyes on her.

The lunar shuttle had just completed the trip from Earth with its cargo of people, supplies, tech and large quantities of things that just couldn't be made on the Moon. It was the lifeline that tripped back and forth from one of Earth's orbiting asteroid space stations. These were connected to the land with elevators that ran up and down a nano-fibre connection, meaning that there was no need for rockets to help people and cargo leave the Earth's gravitational pull[1].

Xalata's trip had begun the day before as she left her home to come and join Brett Orbit, her father, at the Hydroponics Department of the Moon's Central Air Facility and she had no idea of the danger that she would face during the next few weeks - danger that would threaten not just her, but all of the Lunar colony.

Following the journey, she'd been put through the indignities of security at Arrivals, where screening made sure that infected travellers, terrorists and illegal imports of potentially dangerous goods could not gain access to the fragile spaceworld of LunarBase.

Now, though, she was angry as she saw the person meeting her; angry because he wasn't her Dad, angry because he looked creepy and most of all, angry because he didn't look like the sort of person she had imagined on the LunarBase.

"Zala-taar ... my dear..."

"It's 'Zah-latta', not 'Zala-taar'," she broke in "and I'm not your dear. I thought Dad was going to meet me."

---

[1] An idea that had been thought up by a science fiction writer, Arthur C. Clarke, hundreds of years before.

"Unavoidably detained, I'm afraid. The demands of his work, you know. My name is Adolf – like A-dolf but pronounced Ay-dolf, as you can hear – see we have something in common already! I volunteered to meet you – to welcome you to Luna and help you get settled in."

Fark's voice dripped with unsettling tones that made Xalata's skin crawl. She knew that she had to make a good impression – not one of her strengths generally – but she also knew that more than a few minutes alone with this creep would be enough to ensure that she completely blew it before she'd even begun. Summoning the best resources she could, she set her face in as genuine a smile as she could manage – supreme effort – and followed Fark as he led the way into the Arrivals area of LunarBase Nearside – the main hub for anyone visiting the Moon.

Xalata had been living with an aunt on Earth while her father followed the big opportunities on the Moon and earned enough to keep her at a good academy for her initial education. Earth was not a great place to be - a massive pandemic, "The Great Plague", had made normal life almost impossible around fifty years previously. Normal medicines had not stopped the advance of the superbug that had cut a swathe across the world and reduced its population by one third - in some places, wiping out entire towns and cities, leaving no one alive.

So survivors of that period had settled themselves in secure and easily defended areas - mostly on islands such as Britannia, Madeira, Malta and the Indies, or in huge walled cities that had been built to defend their inhabitants: Beijing in China, New Chicago on the borders of the US with Canada and Dubai, in the Arabian Gulf. Border controls were strict and there was lock-down of any area that showed signs of the disease.

Terrorists had also used the virus as a weapon, infecting citizens in undefended cities and causing widespread terror, panic buying and isolation among cities' residents. Those unlucky enough to be outside had a high chance of contracting the disease and of death. Normal life inside the enclaves was much as before, but simply locked down and restricted.

Now, though, was the time when Xalata needed to make some choices about what she wanted to do. When she reached fourteen, her father had encouraged her to come out to LunarBase to learn hydroponics – growing plants without any soil and making breathable air, as there was no atmosphere on the Moon. Frankly, the idea bored her, but she'd had enough of life on Earth, her friends – such as they were – irritated her and the idea of an adventure to the Moon captured her imagination more than anything else had managed to do over the years.

She was quite tall for her age - 14 years and four months old - a tricky age. As she'd come from Earth, she was still wearing Earth clothes, although she'd had to wear a pressure suit for part of the journey. She stood now in the Arrivals area, wearing her black and red-flashed ScramSuit - a one-piece travel outfit - and faux leather boots with brightly coloured titanium buckles - her very favourites. Pretty, in an angry sort of way, she had clear blue eyes and dark spiky hair that stood out from her head in a series of angles.

So here she was with not much idea of what to expect on the Moon and a chip on her shoulder the size of the Zandos building in New London. And Fark was already frying her wiring with his oily manner.

"We'll take the TransTrak across to your accommodation," said Fark, "and your things will follow in a little while."

"OK – but when do I get to see my Dad?" She was getting techy now.

"That will depend on his duty period. Most people finish at around 18 hours, Earth time. Meanwhile, let me look after you..."

Fark was a short and skinny man of about forty Earth years, with lank, greasy hair that flopped across his eyes. His pointed nose and wet lips made him look vaguely like a burrowing animal. He wore the uniform of business people everywhere - dark trousers, white open-neck shirt with a pointed collar, fitted blue jacket and shiny dark blue shoes.

He rubbed his hands together as he talked, one hand on top of the back of the other, reminding Xalata of a bad waiter in a sleazy restaurant she had once visited with her aunt.

"I can take care of myself...", Xalata bit her lip, "well, I mean, that's very kind of you, Mr Fark..."

"A-dolf, please."

"Yes. Sorry, A-dolf. That's kind, very kind. But really there is no need to trouble yourself. If you can take me to the habitat then I can settle in by myself."

She could see that Fark was not impressed. His moist lips set into a thin line and he flicked his unusually long, oily hair back, away from his eyes.

"I see. Very well." And he marched off with big strides (for a small man), leaving Xalata to scamper in his wake, as the last thing she needed was to lose him until she arrived at her new home.

The TransTrak boarding was only a few hundred metres from where they had arrived and Fark quickly identified the correct set of pods that were heading to Xalata's habitat.

Making conversation to ensure that no one could accuse her of being tricky, moody or difficult (regular descriptions from her teachers and keepers on Earth), she said: "I haven't seen anything like the TransTrak before, Mr F ... erm, Adolf, A-dolf – sorry! On Earth we're using trains and travelators."

"Ah yes – not really practical here on the Moon. Low gravity and the lack of an atmosphere make it difficult to travel on the surface. So we've become like worms, my dear, worms! Nanobots create new tunnels to each habitat, as they are built – it's really very quick indeed. A typical tunnel between two points – say of 50 kilometres – can be cut, lined and prepared by the 'bots in under two months. When it's finished, they just stop – part of their clever programming. Now, we can flash through these tunnels in a pod and no one steps on the surface."

As he spoke, the pod in which they had sat, with around ten other people started to move and, as it left the boarding unit, it quickly gained speed until everything outside the windows was simply a blur. It was silent – maglev, magnetic levitation, Xalata guessed – and there was no sense of motion after the initial acceleration.

"So what happens if the nanobots don't stop tunnelling?" asked Xalata, continuing the conversation in the hope that she could get Fark's mind back onto holding forth about stuff and stop him from looking at her.

"Well of course that did happen in the early days. Programming for the 'bots was still not perfected and the termination override on one project failed to engage and the 'bots continued to tunnel right around the Moon's circumference. They only stopped when they reached their starting point because, for the first time, there was nothing left to tunnel. Awful stew about that in the Praesidium – it should never have happened. But then people started to realize that we now had a complete lunar circumnavigable tunnel system – by accident. Not that we use it."

"But don't the 'bots run out of power?"

"No my dear – never. They create their own power from the resources they find in the material around them, just like they do with the building materials. Everything is made from what's there already. On the Moon, we can only make things with what we have. So the imagers – "dupers" I think you young people call them – print new objects and devices from the materials that we have here – rock, minerals and chemicals that we can extract from the surface."

"So, ultimately, the 'bots can go on forever and so can the dupers?"

"Well yes and ... oh, here we are. 20 kilometres in a matter of moments!"

The pod decelerated sharply and pulled into a disembarkation area and, as they moved to step out onto the platform, Fark turned to Xalata:

"You need to play nicely with me, young lady. I can make life very unpleasant if I am so minded," and with that strode off again to the exit, Xalata following behind. A sense of loneliness enveloped her and, for a moment, she wished she had never left the comfort of Earth, but she pulled herself together and chased after Fark down the seemingly endless white tunnels.

If she had know what was to come in the next few weeks, her panic would have seemed mild and her loneliness, just an irritation.

Chapter Two

The habitat was bigger than she had expected. A large clear atrium, like a glass bubble, swept overhead, covering a mall area with shops, entertainment and eateries, just like on Earth. From the sides of the atrium, tunnels pitched underground, labelled with street names – Victoria Road, New York Drive, London Avenue. As far as Xalata could see, they bore no resemblance to the roads she knew on Earth. Each tunnel was formed of crystalline stone – a little like marble but without any colours other than a bland, off-white. Thinking about it, she realized it was the same as the walls of the tunnel for the TransTrak:

The 'bots again, she mused. They set off down Victoria Road and after an initial slope downwards for about 10 or 20 metres, the surface levelled off and the tunnel stretched out before them.

"So, if you want natural light, you need to go back to the mall, then?" she questioned Fark.

"No, indeed. There is more light available in each home within the habitat – you'll see in a few minutes. There is always a lightdome that brings in natural light, usually in the main living area. You can imagine that, with the habitats being largely underground, we have to restrict the amount of surface that is exposed to the vacuum of space. A breach on any lightdome would of course be fatal to those living in there, within only a few minutes. So you'll discover that there are airlock overrides which close quickly in the event of a breach anywhere in the habitat."

"Pretty freakin' gloomy, if you ask me." As she spoke, she thought of Fark's words as they disembarked the pod. "It's very kind of you Mr ... A-dolf," she corrected herself, "to tell me all about the habitat 'n' everything. I'm sure it'll be great once I get used to it."

"Well, let's see how you like this then," said Fark as he pushed through a swinging airlock door that was covered in signs warning about its sudden closure in an emergency. "Your home is just down here and Brett will be along very soon I am sure."

The smaller corridor now led to a number of doors to the left and right, but the one Fark approached was at the very end, facing down the way they had come. On the door, which looked like wood but felt like cool plastic, was a nameplate with "Orbit" in simple print upon it.

"Your key," said Fark and he handed Xalata a small plastic disk about the size of a large coin. As he did so, the door opened automatically. "It only works for you," he continued. "It's hard-wired with your DNA so that, when you approach, the door will open for you and only you. If someone else tries to use it, not only will the key fail, an alert will sound and the area will lock down. So, don't share it!"

"OK," said Xalata. "Sounds a bit overkill."

"Indeed not, my dear. Security is a major priority here. Although privately owned by corporations, the habitats and the work that goes on here are highly guarded. You will learn that in some ways this may restrict your life occasionally. It's all for the greater good."

Xalata walked through the door into a small lobby from which opened a number of other doors.

"I'll leave you here," said Fark. "Your father will no doubt be back in due course, but your luggage will also arrive. Open the door when it arrives, but do not let anyone else inside. Establish first that people are who they say they are."

"OK – er, thanks," said Xalata and she stood by the door as Fark walked out.

"Anything, my dear. Anything at all. You have only to ask," he said as he turned on his heel and walked away.

Xalata watched him go and suddenly felt very alone and rather scared. Here she was on the Moon for Frank's sake! The only person she knew was Fark, and her Dad would return, who knew when? She decided to explore – a job that wouldn't take very long.

The home consisted of the entrance lobby, a utility cupboard containing equipment for cleaning, a small living area and kitchen/diner with – yes, a lightdome - a bathroom with a shower, loo and hand basin and two tiny bedrooms – one with a small double bed and the other with two bunks.

Everywhere was light and off-white and there was no sense of a personality about the place. It could have as easily been a prison on Earth as a home on the Moon. In many ways though, it was better than Xalata had expected. What *had* she expected? She couldn't really recall, but all she felt was a big sense of displacement – being somewhere totally alien to her.

Her thoughts were interrupted by a sharp buzz and she realized that it must be a visitor at the door. She went back into the lobby and saw a flashing red light on a speaker grille near the door. On a tiny screen she could see an image of the person outside – no sign of Xalata's bags. In fact, the visitor was a young girl, about her age.

"Hello," she said to the microphone, pressing what she assumed was the intercom button. No. It was the door release and, a moment later, she was facing the girl on the doorstep.

"Hi," said the girl.

"Um, hey. Who are you?"

"I'm Melody and I live next door. Your dad told me you would be arriving. I saw you through the viewport – you were with Fark, weren't you?"

"Yep. I've just arrived," said Xalata, pointlessly. Melody was quite small and, although she was by no means overweight, she carried a little more than she was happy with. She had a lively face that was set off by short-cropped hair that gave her a rather boyish look. Her eyes were deep brown, almost black and the size of them, coupled with her short hair made her look rather elf-like. She was wearing a ScramSuit, similar in style to Xalata's but with muted grey colours that seemed to blend into the background and on her feet were dull and practical boots, also in grey.

"So, won't you ask me in? Or did Fark give you the 'Trust nobody. Invite no one in' spiel?"

"Er, yeah."

"Tell you what then, come to my place instead," and she pointed two doors further down the corridor.

"My dad may be home soon – won't he think it a bit funny if I'm not here?"

"Not really," said Melody. "He'll know where you are."

Chapter Three

Melody's home was almost identical to the one they had just left with one difference: there was a lived-in feel to the place. Some pictures of places on Earth were stuck onto the walls, there were some personal bits and pieces around the living area and, in the corner near to the kitchen area there was a guitar, propped into a corner beside the work surface.

"Do you play?" asked Xalata as she drifted around the living space.

"Sure," said Melody, "I've been learning guitar for about four years and I'm covering loads of songs by Marlene Thripp and Ent Quory. Do you play any instruments?"

"Nope. Never learned. Never wanted to. I tried to learn keyboard once, back at home, but I was hopeless and gave up after a couple of lessons." She flopped down on one of the chairs and looked around the room. "Not much of a place to live, really, is it?"

Melody shook her head,

"I don't agree with you. I like it here. I've been here since I was four years old..."

"And how old are you now?"

"Same age as you, fourteen."

"How in Frank's name do you know so much about me?"

"Your dad talks about you all the time. He's really made up that you're coming to stay here. He's missed you like crazy."

"Dad's not seen me for years."

"Exactly," said Melody. "You can guess it's a big deal for him that you've got on the shuttle and come up here."

"I s'pose. There wasn't much other option back home. I was living with my aunt and she ... well, I'm not the easiest person to get on with. Not sure why I'm telling you that. I can be spiky – I just get fried about stupid things. Everyone seems stupid. Add to that living in a compound because of the disease everywhere..."

"Hmm," said Melody, "I think it's part of our age. My mum always says that I'm *going through a phase*, but to me, I'm with you. Everyone else is dim."

"Yeah. And don't get me started about boys," continued Xalata, "what's that all about? Will they ever grow up? Hitting things, breaking things, pratting around as soon as a girl shows up. Mind you, they're just as bad when they're on their own, as far as I can see. Anyway, why are you in this place? I'm here because I couldn't get on with my aunt any longer."

"Bit different for me," said Melody. "Mum and I have lived on LunarBase since I was four. My dad died in an accident at work here. Mum's an astro-scientist and she works on stuff for the Praesidium to..."

"You're the second person that's said that word. What's the *Praesidium*?" asked Xalata.

"It's the local government on the Moon. Each habitat area has councillors who then represent us at the main Praesidium headquarters at LunarBase – where you arrived on the shuttle. The Praesidium building was originally one of the first habitats created and they revamped it so that it became government offices."

"OK – um, sorry 'bout your dad. That must have been terrible."

"Not really. I was too young to know what was going on. I hardly saw him and I can't really remember him other than from movies and photos that my mum showed me."

"So what's she do for her work, then?"

"Well, I'm not sure," said Melody. "It's all secret stuff to do with developing our presence here on the Moon. I think it's the same old thing – someone else wants a bit of what we are doing and we have to try and stop them."

"Like what?" said Xalata. "I mean, I know there's mining and stuff goes on up here and that we are using the Moon as a place to jump off to the other planets. Surely there's enough to go around?"

"You'd have to ask my mum. And she probably won't tell you anything because of security. That's one of the reasons this place is locked down so tight." Her face brightened and lost its serious cast, "You want a drink or something?"

"Yeah, I'd kill a juice."

"We've got synth juice but it's not great. Other than that, there's cola, water and coffee."

"Oh, great. I live on juice. OK – water please ... er, thanks."

Melody moved into the kitchen area, drew off two glasses of water from a tap and brought them over.

Xalata drank thirstily and, after wiping her mouth said,

"So what's your mum's name?"

"Dawn. Dawn Fret. *Pioneer in lunar habitats*. That's what she signs herself as. She's been doing lunar stuff since she graduated. Dad was doing the same as her, but of course that all fell apart and so she had to make it work – can't have been easy with a four-year old and a heavy job."

"Similar story," said Xalata. "Dad couldn't cope with me after my mother left us. Not sure when she went – just disappeared. He works in the Air Supply division of Lunar Hydroponics and I think he wouldn't have wanted to deal with me at all if things hadn't gone offline between me and my aunt. Shame, cos I really like her, but she just fries me. Mind you, most people fry me. So Dad's going to have to put up with me, I guess. I'm off to the Academy to learn hydroponics..."

"I know," said Melody. "That's great because I'm doing the same course. You'll start same time as me."

"Well, at least I'll know someone!" laughed Xalata, "Wow – first time I've felt like laughing since I got here. Thanks for coming round to the door when I arrived, it's..."

But she had no time to complete the sentence. The door chime sounded and Melody went to the intercom:

"It's your Dad," she said, and pressed the door release to let him in.

Chapter Four

Xalata's dad, Brett Orbit, stood in the entry not quite sure what to do. He'd not seen her for nearly a year, as he had gone without holiday to ensure that his projects were completed. Guilty feelings? You bet and they were written all over his face as he saw his daughter sitting in the living room of his neighbour's home.

"Hi Xally. Um. My, how you've grown," he laughed nervously.

"For Frank's sake, Dad. You see me on chat most weeks."

"Yeah, sorry. Didn't know what to say. Can I have a hug?"

Xalata crossed the room and hugged her dad. He was only a little taller than her and she felt embarrassed showing emotion in front of Melody, but still, here she was with a new best friend already.

Brett stepped back and looked at her,

"You have actually grown quite a lot – I just see your head and shoulders on chat. It's great to see you, Xally. What do you think to the Moon?"

"Honestly? It's a bit dull. I can't imagine anything exciting happens here," said Xalata with a frown. "What's for dinner?"

"Ah, some things don't change. OK – let's wander back to ours and I'll cook up a great meal I've been saving for you. Pepperoni pizza – I know it's your favourite."

"Yeah, when I was nine perhaps." Then she smiled at him, "OK – sounds good. Let's go – thanks Melody. Great to meet up – I'll catch you around."

With that, Xalata walked out of the door, leaving her dad and Melody to say their goodbyes. She crossed the hall to the door for their home and it opened automatically – the key was in her pocket. As she walked in, she noticed her dad's workbag beside her suitcase. It stood open and there, peeking out from the document folder was an item marked "Eyes only – security one". She was about to take a look when she heard the sound of the door lock disengaging and she moved on into the living area.

Her dad came into the room. He looked tired and he sat down in the chair, looking at Xalata.

"So how was your journey," he asked.

"Fine," said Xalata, "But I can't get my head round how different it is on the Moon. I mean, everything is like top security and you can't just wander around. In fact it feels a bit like a prison. I thought the compounds on Earth were bad enough."

"Sure," said Brett." You'll get used to it."

For a few moments there was silence. Brett and Xalata looked at each other. There was a huge distance between them even though they were in the same room. Xalata looked at the floor. Brett suddenly made a move into the kitchen and began clattering pots as he got together the pizza and prepared for dinner.

"So when do I begin school, dad?" asked Xalata.

"The new academic year begins the day after tomorrow so I guess you'll be going to school then. Melody will be going to the same Academy so you'll be able to go along with her."

"Okay. Do I need stuff? What do I need to take with me?"

"Just your pad. Everything else will be provided."

Xalata looked at her bag, down in the lobby and said,

"Right, I'll set about getting my stuff in place. I assume I'm in here," and she gestured to the doorway on the right.

"Yep, that's the one - make your choice of either bed. They're both made up."

She picked up her bag and pulled it into the room, looking around at the sparse furnishing: a bunk bed, a small side table with a mirror over it, a chair and a wardrobe area with some shelving. Light came from the ceiling, all of which glowed gently. She opened her bag and pulled out some clothes and hung them up, musing all the time about what she had left behind.

She pulled out her pad and looked around for a charging point - there was one beside the bunk - just handy. She quickly discovered the public network - called *The Q*, it was a quantum network that had no boundaries and provided instant communication and access to information and entertainment, wherever you were. So far, it had never been tested beyond the Solar System, but the belief was that it would work instantly, wherever you were in the Universe.

She logged in with her universal ID that had been given to her at birth. Messages pinged and her digest of interests flashed to show that she had news about some of the topics she liked. Time for that later. The smell of pizza was starting to permeate the place and she grinned to herself. She'd been snide in snapping back at Dad so quickly about her food likes - pizza still rang her bell, any time.

She stepped out of the room and there was the pizza, waiting on the table along with a green drink of some sort.

"Thanks Dad," she said, doing her best to give a breezy and cheerful impression.

"Sure you still like it?" he asked.

"I'll force it down somehow," she said and gave her most winning smile. Brett visibly relaxed.

"I thought that maybe you'd gone off it or grown out of it," he said.

"Nah, just being a pain - sorry. I'm not that happy about leaving Earth and this place is a bit of a shock. I'll get used to it," and she took a long pull on the green drink, pulled a wry face and said, "And what's *that*?"

"Synth juice - the best we can do up here. It has all the same nutritional value as..."

"I don't care! It's pretty revolting." She tucked into the pizza. "Tell me about the school."

"Well, it's the Academy for Hydroponics Growers, as you know. You'll travel each day, with Melody, to the Moon's Central Air Facility. It's where I work too, but I'll be leaving earlier than you. The school opens five days a week and you'll be starting the course led by Mr Wiggins - he's the main tutor and most of your time will be spent in his classes and tutorials."

"What's he like?"

"Wiglet? He's OK"

"Who?"

"Wiglet is what everyone calls him except to his face. He's about fifty years old and has had a very elevated career before taking up his teaching post here. He was one of the main founders of the original lunar colony, so he's experienced it from the tough days."

Xalata chewed thoughtfully on the pizza crust.

"So Melody Fret and I will be on the same course together, yes?"

"Yep, that's the plan, unless you find you can't stand each other. Seems unlikely though - she's a nice girl, if a bit nervous."

"What do you mean," said Xalata, recalling the lively girl she had met earlier.

"She puts on a good front, but she's had some bad times and those sometimes cause her to be, well, careful in tricky situations. You'll find she's fine. Not much chance of any danger around here!"

They finished the pizza.

Chapter Five

The news was not good. There had been an attack on a habitat on Farside - the side of the Moon that constantly faces away from the Earth. Contrary to popular belief, it isn't dark on the other side of the Moon - in fact it's just as light as Earth during daytime, when the sun shines on it. The lunar day and night last over 29 Earth days however, Nearside also gets reflected sunlight shone back from the Earth.

The attack had been bizarre - more a wrecking expedition than anything else - on a habitat that was barely populated. An entire section of one of the main arms from the central atrium had been breached with a series of massive holes in the lightdomes and oddly, through the Moon's surface into the underlying tunnels. These had been considered to be almost indestructible, hidden, as they were deep down. But something or someone had used extreme force to create a devastating attack on the pressurised habitat and threaten the people who lived in it.

No one had seen what had caused the attack - some felt it must be a huge vehicle like a terrestrial armoured tank. Others claimed it must be aliens. Yet, whatever or whoever it was, had remained invisible as the residents of the habitat fled for shelter behind the automatic airlocks. Now sealed off, the damaged section of the habitat would remain that way until someone managed to get the repair bots working on the structure.

"What's that about, then Dad?" said Xalata as she chewed her breakfast that morning - a strange composite of hydroponic oats, imported nuts and some fruit that she could not identify. "Will it attack us?"

"Too far away, I think. A vehicle that could inflict that damage would take ages to get around to Nearside. It's probably something to do with one of the extremist groups that are trying to make our lives a misery."

"Such as who?"

But before Brett could answer, the door communicator sounded. Xalata, expecting it to be Melody, rushed to the door - it was Fark.

"Well, good morning, my dear. And have we settled in well?"

"Yeah, well I'm fine thanks, A-dolf," she was pleased she had remembered his name correctly and judging by his leer, so was he.

At that moment, Melody appeared behind Fark and he let her step past.

"Actually, it's good you're here as well, Melody. I have something to say to both of you," said Fark. "The attacks on Farside have raised the security alert for the whole of LunarBase. Therefore, you will need protection - I have been assigned to accompany you to and from school."

"Very kind, A-dolf," said Brett, "don't you think, girls? I'm sure you'll feel safe in his hands." Xalata barely suppressed a shudder and Melody just looked at Xalata without speaking a word.

"So, when you're ready..." said Fark.

The girls shrugged and picked up their bags. With a quick peck on the cheek for her dad, Xalata headed out of the door - still chewing - and followed the rapid progress of Fark with Melody trotting behind. Xalata turned to look back and saw Brett watching them go. She gave a wave and he smiled, waved back and then went into the home.

The TransTrak was crowded and they pushed their way onto the vehicle and found a seat near the back. Fark stood in front of them, looking down at them. The doors closed silently and the train accelerated into the tunnel so that, only a few minutes later, they were disembarking at the Moon's Central Air Facility.

"I know that you already know the way, Melody," said Fark, "but I shall accompany you all the same. Please stay with me in the crowd." He pushed his way forward and they rapidly headed toward the tunnel leading down to the Hydroponics Institute.

"Is he always like this," hissed Xalata to Melody, "I mean, where does he get off? What's he do and why's my dad so keen for him to be with us?"

"He's one of your dad's team. Don't know what he does, but he's certainly taken an interest in you."

"Jeeps! Just the thing, eh. A creepy nerd wants to follow me around - just like home."

"What do you mean?" asked Melody.

"It's just that I had a guy who always wanted to be near me during my last term at school on Earth. I couldn't shake him off. He gave me the shudders and eventually I had to get tough..."

"What did you do?"

"Told him to get lost and that he was the biggest weirdo I knew and to slope off out of my life."

"Ladies." Fark was suddenly beside them. "Having fun? Nice chat? Your college course awaits."

And with an exaggerated bow he indicated the entrance to the Hydroponics Institute and the Academy that was situated inside it.

Chapter Six

The Academy was very, very quiet - unlike any school that Xalata had ever been in. Only a few other students were wandering around and they all seemed absorbed in the pads they carried. The building was essentially a large unit off the main atrium of the LunarBase. Tunnel corridors filtered off left and right as she and Melody walked down towards a classroom and Xalata could gauge no idea of the size of the place.

"It's not actually a classroom as you might know it from your time on Earth," said Melody. "It's more of a study area with occasional teaching sessions - tutorials. We're left to get on with it once we have started, so you're free to work as you think is best."

"Sounds a recipe for hacking off work to me," replied Xalata as they approached a door near the end of the main runway.

The door opened into a large room that was a cross between a library, laboratory and common room. Other students were lounging on the chairs - around twenty in all - and an older man with slightly wild hair and a kindly expression was busy in the lab area with some equipment. As they entered, some of the students acknowledged Melody and turned their interest to Xalata - a new face.

"Hi guys, I'm Xalata," she said and a few of them waved briefly before turning back to their all-absorbing pads. One of them - a gangly boy of about fifteen - stood up and wandered over:

"Hey, Xalata, I'm Glitch. Melody'll tell you all about me. Just think of me as the go-to person for anything you need."

"Oh yeah?" retorted Xalata, "and why would I want to do that? You have something that others here don't have?"

"Yep, I just out-cool 'em. Mistah friggin' Freeze, that's me!"

Xalata folded her arms, cocked her head to one side and did *that* look. All girls know the one. It encompasses disbelief, disdain and dismissal.

"Really?" she said, "and that's the full deal, the total of your offering?"

Glitch smiled knowingly,

"You'll see. Anyway, what brings you to our humble classroom? Have you just come from Earth - you look like an Earther."

"Oh, and what does an Earther look like?"

"Well, you've got a bit of a suntan - don't get that here. Your clothes don't look like the ones we can get from the outlets on LunarBase and you haven't had the haircut yet."

Xalata looked around. Nearly everyone had short or very short hair - she'd not really noticed. Her spiky hairstyle stood out like a sore thumb.

"OK - so why the shorties in the hair department then?" she said.

"It's style," replied Glitch, "Style with a capital "Stuh"."

The look returned to Xalata's face.

"Yeah? Really? If that's style then I'm from Mars."

"Hey, Martian!" Glitch snapped back. "Welcome to Moon!"

"Give over, Glitch. You're being a pain," said Melody. "Just ignore him. The real reason we all have rubbish hair is that there are no stylists up here. Essential personnel only. Hair and beauty doesn't come into it, so we have to make do with what we have."

"OK - I can cope with that," said Xalata, thinking *For Frank's sake, a quarter of a million miles from home and you can't get your hair cut?* Her face brightened, "OK yep, no problem. Just have to be creative, I guess?"

At this point, the tutor with the wild hair came over.

"Hello, Xalata. Your father told me you would be joining us today - welcome. I see you've already met Mr Shaw-Storey..."

"Who?" said Xalata.

"Ah, he'll have introduced himself as Glitch, of course. Justin Shaw-Storey is his name."

At this, Glitch ambled back to the seats where he had come from, looking over his shoulder with a grin.

"My name is Mr Wiggins. I'm the bio tutor and a good part of your hydroponics course will take place here and in the culture areas behind the Academy. You'll need to get yourself kitted out with lab wear, the instrument kits and so on. I'm sure Melody will help you sort those out. Our first group tutorial today is not until midday, so I hope you'll be able to sort out the kit before then, from the Student Commissary. If you need anything else, any help or guidance, Melody may be your best bet. However, don't hesitate to come and talk to me - I'm here most of the time."

His glasses - so old-fashioned - wobbled on the end of his nose as he looked over them and talked to Xalata. She felt comfortable with the thought of him as her tutor and so she responded brightly:

"Thanks Mr Wiggins. I'm sure I'll fit in quickly. I'm looking forward to starting the hydroponics course..." and to herself she said, *You liar. Nothing's further from the truth. This will bore you to death.*

Mr Wiggins pointed out some of the features of the room and then wandered back to his workstation. Melody and Xalata watched him go:

"He's OK," said Melody. "Everyone here likes him, apart from Rose and Penny, that is."

"Oh, and who are they?"

"Check out in the corner by the instrument shelves."

At the back of the room, sitting together and with no other companions were two girls of about the same age as Xalata and Melody. One was very strikingly good-looking, despite the hairstyle. The other was much less appealing - a harsh face with a spiteful look and an aggressive attitude.

"Wow, who are those two?" said Xalata.

"Rose Pretty and Penny Wrath," replied Melody. "They're the misfits. Rose is the pretty one and she really thinks she's pretty by name, pretty by nature. She isn't. Penny is fairly much how she looks. She's a thorn in everyone's side. If there's trouble, she and Rose will almost always be right at the front of it. I'd stay away from them, if you can."

Inevitably, as Melody was speaking, the infamous pair caught Xalata looking across the room at them.

"Oi!" shouted Rose, "who you staring at?"

Xalata raised her eyebrows and looked away.

"I'm talking to you, new girl,"

The sound of boots on the floor of the classroom heralded the arrival of Rose Pretty, followed quickly by Penny Wrath.

"Oh, hi," said Xalata sweetly. "How nice of you to welcome me to the Academy. I'm Xalata, by the way. And you must be...?"

"Never mind who we are," said Penny, "you need to watch your mouth."

"I do? And why is that?

"Because," said Rose, "people with too much to say usually end up eating their words. Do I make myself clear?"

"Actually, no," said Xalata, "I'm really not very bright. Perhaps you could spell it out for me?"

Mr Wiggins approached and Rose and Penny backed off, pretending they had just been chatting.

"Have you started your assignments, Rose and Penny?" he said. "I seem to remember that you're rather behind with them."

"Sure, Mr Wiggins, we were just saying hello to Xala-taar, here."

"Xa-latta, please ladies," said Xalata with exaggerated friendliness.

"Whatever," they muttered and walked back to their corner, Mr Wiggins following them at a distance.

"Don't fry them, Xalata," said Melody. "They can make serious trouble."

"Ask me how worried I am," said Xalata.

"Er, how worried are you?"

Xalata snapped her fingers.

"Oh," said Melody. "OK - let's get your stuff from the Commissary."

The traveller moves on

Its movement through space is silent. On the surface of Mars, preparations are being made for the impact - this is the first of five live asteroids programmed to hit the planet.

Meanwhile, elsewhere on the surface, greenhouse gas factories are churning out vast quantities of CO_2 and methane as well as a cocktail of other chemicals that, on Earth, are prohibited because of their effect on global warming. The free-flowing water on the surface of Mars has been brought to the surface and bacteria introduced to enable plant growth through advanced hydroponics - the soil is not yet present that will allow plants to grow on their own. As these technologies all work together, so the atmosphere is growing gently, day by day, but the whole process will take years before the atmosphere is breathable.

The asteroid's progress is monitored by automatic systems both on board the space rock itself and at monitoring stations on Mars, the Earth and the Moon. This is a dangerous manoeuvre - nothing like it has ever been attempted before outside the realms of science fiction.

Fusion engines correct the flight path in small increments, adjusting the trajectory to ensure impact will be where and when it is planned.

Then...

An engine fires and the huge asteroid, step by tiny step, hour by hour, swings through microscopic diversions from its original course, on an arc that sets it on a new target.

Chapter Seven

"How was the first day?" said Brett as he walked into the home at the end of work.

"OK, I guess," replied Xalata who was sitting in the lounge area, trying to figure out an assignment that she had been given by Mr Wiggins. "The Academy is OK and it was good that I knew Melody. Met a few other types who were OK too, apart from a couple of real aliens..."

"Let me guess, Rose and Penny," said Brett.

"Right on the nose. What a couple of idiots. Tried to come the heavy with me and I thought, nothing to lose here. So just ignored them."

"Watch out for those two," said Brett. "They're trouble. Rose has only held onto her place at the Academy because she's actually a brilliant student. Penny's there because … of a number of reasons … but mainly that her father is in the Praesidium."

"Well, anyway, they can do their thing and keep out of my way. Talking of being in the way ... Fark. Does he really have to accompany us? It's not as if we're special - why would anyone target us? What's the danger anyway?"

Brett explained to Xalata about the attacks on Farside and told her about a shadowy religious group called the Asttarians who believe that Lunar exploration and exploitation are against the will of Asttar, their god, whom they believe brought original life to Earth from space.

"Now, it doesn't matter that you might think their views are crazy, these guys have friends in high places and the security council of the Praesidium is putting all the military on high alert because of what the Asttarians might do next."

"And what might that be, do they know?" said Xalata.

Brett shook his head. "Their leader is a guy called Frank Wordsmith. He's based somewhere on Earth - no one really knows where - and his mission is to keep the faith pure, in other words, stop people from leaving it or messing about with it. He also wants to recruit as many people to the Asttarians as possible - there are some big incentives for them: they all look after each other as a huge extended family; those who are young and earning money pay large amounts to the Church of Asttar every month and that subsidises those who are older and can't work. But also, people who don't have work - who've been left on the sidelines by society, they are of interest to the Asttarians too and Wordsmith is making sure that he pulls them into the fold because they will do exactly what he tells them, because they rely on him."

"OK - I don't see the connection with Farside and the attack on the habitat."

"That's classic Asttarian. They stage a set-piece attack or disruption, but they don't claim it. They like to leave people wondering. I'll bet you've never heard of them."

"Nope - but I don't take notice of the newsfeeds anyway."

"You will, soon enough. The Asttarians are growing rapidly and they have a popular following among people of your age, all of whom are sworn to secrecy..."

"So how do *you* know about it?" said Xalata. "I mean, if they're so darned hidden, how come you can tell me all about this?"

"You asked about Fark. He's the senior security officer for the LunarBase. He works with my team to keep us safe. I'm telling you this because I know about it and I want to protect you. You need to keep this information close - don't share it at the Academy. Melody is aware too as her mother works in a similar area to me. However, I suggest you don't discuss it in public. You're safe enough here at home or at Melody's. Now, what would you like to eat?"

"Well, pizza ... of course!"

Chapter Eight

"Hey, Zala-taar! Still taking the ugly pills?"

Penny Wrath had been leaning behind an airlock door as Xalata headed in for classes the next morning. She sneered at Melody and lurched at Xalata, as if to push into her.

"Back off, Penny. Messing with me is not a good idea."

"Ha!" Penny pushed her face close to Xalata's, "Scared. So scared. I'll run away now." And with a final scowl she headed off towards the classroom.

"Is she going to keep turning up like that," said Xalata to Melody.

"Yeah, I'm afraid so. She always turns up - it's why we call her Bad Penny. Erm, I don't call her that to her face..."

"Why not - she's just a bully. You need to stand up to her."

"I can't. I don't know how and it frightens me when you challenge her like that."

"What's she going do? Fight me? Attack me and try to kill me? Nah, I don't think so. It's all too locked down here - she'd be discovered and dealt with very quickly. She's just trying to psych us out. Bad Penny? Psycho Penny more like."

Melody laughed, a little nervously and they headed off for the classroom.

The tutorials were surprisingly interesting, Xalata found. The science of hydroponics is all about growing food in water, without soil - very important on a hostile terrain such as the Moon or indeed any other planet. The Moon is important in the further exploration of the Solar System because it is a good staging post for visiting the planets. The low gravity means that landings and take-off are relatively simple but the hostile environment - no atmosphere, no protection from deadly radiation - means that people on the Moon needed to live in habitats.

The first ones that had been created, many years earlier, had been very primitive with living conditions little better than those on the space stations that had orbited the Earth in the 20th and 21st century. Now the habitats were much more comfortable, with individual living quarters and, thanks to artificial gravity, the general feel of the place resembled living in an extended shopping mall on Earth. More importantly, the negative effects of low gravity on the human body were reduced. Cracking the gravity issue had been the biggest achievement in space exploration to date and the technology that was used on LunarBase was also used on all the space vehicles that travelled between the planets.

That day's tutorial was a look at mineral nutrients that needed to be in water that was used to grow hydroponic food. Mr Wiggins sat in the meeting area of the room and the students clustered around him on comfortable chairs, watching the display screen that occupied the far wall.

"So, our culture medium must be protected from light, as you know ... don't you Rose?"

"Of course, Mr Wiggins," said Rose who had been talking behind her hand to Penny. "If we don't keep out the light from the growing medium, algae can form and disrupt the growing process. That's also why we keep the nutrient circulating, so that it has less time exposed to the air and to light."

"Very good, Penny," said Mr Wiggins, "And I think you should all now check out the overview of the nutrient sets that are more commonly used - I'll ping you the page location shortly. After that, I'd like your views on which nutrients might most suitably be used for peas, beans or other pulses - and can we try to be a bit original? Be ready with your responses to me by end of day tomorrow. I expect a two minute tri-V from each of you in my inbox please."

"I don't know how Rose does it," said Melody as the class broke up. "She doesn't pay attention and most of the time she's just fooling about with Penny."

"My dad says that she's very bright," said Xalata. "Probably true but she still fries my wiring. Let's get the page from Wiglet and then we can get this work out of the way, what do you think? Anyway, what's a tri-V?"

"It's a *viva voce video*, three v's - I think it's Latin, you send in your two-minute report as a video so you can add presentation content or call in stuff from The Q. It's better than writing it and he can check that you've done it and that you've understood what you're saying. It stops people just copying chunks of text and putting them as their own stuff." said Melody.

"OK - schools down on Earth haven't caught up with that idea yet - we still mail assignments to be marked - some people even print them!"

"Yeah, well you can't do that here - paper is practically non-existent!"

At that moment, Glitch sauntered over and flopped onto a seat beside them.

"Hey gang, how's the intellectual pursuit? What's with the intense academic chat, friends? Let's freeze-frame, huh? Fancy a cooler?"

"Oh hi, Glitch - or should I say, Justin?" teased Xalata.

"Well, yeah, not keen on Justin. Glitch is my handle - sort of never forgiven the parents, really."

"OK - so, a cooler?" said Xalata.

"Sure," replied Glitch, let's see what delights have been cooked up in the drinks department," and, with that he set off to the kitchen area where a small drinks vending machine sat waiting. "OK - we've got beetroot, tomato, or cucumber juice. What's happened to the citrus?"

"Crop failed," a voice called across the room. Melody was still studying her pad and had overheard the conversation. "They had an infection in the reservoir in the orangery and they've had to wipe the whole lot. Plenty of ordinary water though!"

As Xalata and Glitch pondered their choice of drink, Melody returned to her pad.

"Oh no, Jupe's loops! Take a look at this guys,"

She switched her pad to display on the far wall screen. A video report from the local news agency was showing some footage from a security camera:

"Recently discovered evidence of the creature or machine behind the Farside devastation at Habitat 14 has been backed up by video from a private security camera. All others appeared to have been disabled during the attack, but this one has captured some indistinct images of what went on..."

As the students all gathered around, a strange creature met their eyes. It was big – slug-shaped, but the size of an old London double-decker bus, but with a strange opalescent carapace. It appeared to crawl, but actually had a series of small stumpy legs that allowed it to propel itself across the terrain very quickly. It was darting around the habitat and was destroying the environment - clouds of dust raced into space as the dome of the habitat shattered under its force. The fact that it had opened itself to the vacuum of space - something that would kill a normal creature - seemed not to bother it at all.

As it went out of the camera's range, a whole panel of walling appeared to dissolve in front of it.

"For Frank's sake, what in the name of all that's ugly is *that*?" cried Rose from the other side of the room.

As if to answer her question, the reporter on the piece continued,

"And here we have security chief, A-dolf Fark. Whatever is this thing?"

Fark's leering visage peered down from the screen,

"It appears to be some sort of Cryomorph. These were engineered originally to aid construction and also for defence - as a fighting machine it is irresistible and invincible. The technologies to develop it have all been created as part of the Lunar colonization, but no one has ever had access to them. I have to say also that this particular Cryomorph is exceptionally large. Normally, Cryomorph are relatively small. This one also appears to have much more destructive capacity than the ones we have created in the past. Metals appear to be dissolving in front of it, suggesting some sort of acid facility and there appear also to be huge jolts of power that are being used to blast through structures that would normally resist such a creature."

"But who's created this thing, if we haven't?" said the reporter.

"A good question," said Fark, *"and one I cannot answer at the moment. However, we are all aware of the threat posed by certain groups that wish us not to be here on the Moon..."*

"You mean the Asttarians?"

"I couldn't comment on that, but sufficient to say that my security teams are going to be tightening up our environment significantly."

"Is that necessary?" said the reporter, *"This is all taking place on Farside, surely? Does Nearside have to be affected?"*

"I'm sure you realize that with molecular technologies and the power of nanotech, amazing things can be achieved in relatively little time. I would not rule out the possibility that an illicit operation that wishes us ill is already planning its attacks across the habitats. Vigilance is most important."

"Well, that was A-dolf Fark, security chief for LunarBase, from Nearside ... " The reporter's voice got lost in the hubbub of chatter from the students.

"Ladies and gentlemen," Mr Wiggins' voice cut through the noise. "I'm sure you're most anxious about the news, but you do have your studies to consider. I don't believe there is any immediate danger - our alert status is currently on green - so please settle down and get back to your tasks. This term will finish quickly enough without us leaving gaps in the curriculum."

And, so saying, he disappeared down to the lab area.

Chapter Nine

Back at the home, the mood was sombre. Brett appeared distracted and Xalata was edgy.

"So what's going to happen, Dad?" she said after several minutes of silence.

"I really don't know, love. These attacks are becoming more dangerous and I think that this creature - what was it called...?"

"Cryomorph..."

"This creature is fairly much unstoppable with anything we have on LunarBase. We have weapons of course - it would be mad not to. But the power of that thing..." His voice died off and he went back into a reflective mood.

"Shall I make something for us to eat?" said Xalata.

"Hmm...?"

"Food? Something to eat? Come on Dad, snap out of it."

Brett looked genuinely startled, "Sorry, Xally. This is just getting to me. The whole thing feels wrong. How has this *thing* been created and yet no one knows anything about it? Yes, food - great idea. We're fresh out of pizza, but as you've had it three days running, I guess that's no bad thing."

"I'll make up some stir-fry," said Xalata. "That's easy and the one thing I've learned on the Moon is that there's no shortage of beansprouts!"

Bill laughed. "After ten years, the novelty of them fades. Still, good and healthy, huh?"

Xalata rattled the wok, pulled out some supplies of ingredients and began the process of cooking up a storm. Within minutes the home was filled with the aroma of fast-fried beansprouts, peppers, onions and tofu with a handful of dried organic noodles thrown in for good measure.

As they sat and ate, Xalata revisited the topic:

"Why are they doing this Dad? What's the point and what are they trying to achieve?"

"It's terror tactics," replied Brett. "They want to frighten people away from the Moon because they see this as a sacred place. Asttar apparently came from the Moon - a load of old space junk, to my mind. But some people will hang on to improbable ideas just because it makes them feel more secure. This Frank Wordsmith guy is stirring up a storm among people who don't have much to live for - it's classic for a belief system like this. So, they want to return the Moon to its pre-colonisation state: no people, no habitats, no enterprise or space-hopping, using it as a base..."

"So what about the planets, then?" said Xalata. "Do they have the same feelings about Mars, for instance? I know we're terraforming there."

"Not sure really, Xally. Their message changes to fit the context. If they can stir up people's passions with a cause to fight for, then it doesn't much matter whether it makes any sense or not. Hey, that stir-fry is great. You can stay! I'll clear when we are done - do you have any homework?"

"Yeah, I have to do a tri-V - you heard of that?"

"Of course - it's standard practice in all courses at your level. Didn't they use that at the Academy on Earth?"

"Never - not even heard of it. Mind you, that place and tech. Just didn't get it. I'll sort it out - can I ask if I need any help?"

"Of course, you know I'll always try my best to help you with anything you need."

With that, Xalata headed for her bedroom and folded down the small desk and illuminated the screen. Without thinking, she tapped into the news feed again and was surprised to see an imposing looking man, haranguing a group of reporters:

"The Words are the Words of Asttar. The Will is the Will of Asttar. The Way is the Way of Asttar. Hear the Words. Bow down to the Will. Follow the Way."

He seemed quite out of it, with a tiny fleck of foam appearing at one corner of his mouth. His white hair was swept back and fell on either side of his face. He had a long straight nose and perfect white teeth. As he shouted, he gesticulated, almost like a conductor of an orchestra, urging people to follow his direction.

"Your ways are not the ways of Asttar. Your deeds are foul in the sight of Asttar. He will revenge himself. He will bring down nations and peoples with the might of his thunder. His power is everywhere. His sight is everywhere. He is everywhere and his followers are those who tread the right path."

The reporters looked uncomfortable as the man - Frank Wordsmith, as the screen caption said - ranted and raved in front of them.

"Er, Mr Wordsmith," one reporter ventured, *"Do Asttarians have anything to do with the trouble on LunarBase Farside?"*

"The unbelievers who have committed sacrilege on the sacred Moon," Wordsmith's voice suddenly dropped to a sinister whisper, *"will fall beneath the might of Asttar. Asttar will revenge himself on those whose own greed has led them to deface that holy place."*

"So the answer's 'yes' then?"

"Asttar speaks, not through his humble servant, but through his actions. Fear the might of Asttar! Fear the retribution that is to follow!"

The screen report cut away to some talking heads commenting on the news and Xalata switched away from it.

He's looped, she thought, *and I'm right here on the target of his insanity: The Moon! 'It's gonna be a bumpy ride!' Where did that come from? Jupe's, that's from a book Dad used to read me years back when we were all together on Earth. That seems so long ago.*

She, her mum and dad had been in a small village in the UK, just between Birmingham and Manchester - spaceport cities that were paving the way to the planets. She remembered a life where the days seemed long, the sun shone and her parents were happy, in the days before the Great Epidemic. Her mother with long, dark hair; her dad, tall and good-looking and relaxed. Those days were long gone by.

She mused on her predicament for a few moments before pulling herself together and getting together the materials for her Tri-v.

Chapter Ten

Meanwhile, across the lobby in Melody's home, there were sighs of frustration and squeaks of despair coming from the living area. Melody was seated, with her guitar in her lap, peering at her pad where she was trying to improve a song.

"It's just no friggin' good! I simply can't get it." She replayed a section of the song from the tutor on her pad.

Once again, she struck up the chords on her guitar and began to sing. Her voice was clear, with a bit of edge and she sang well, but suddenly the same sequence of chords defied her fingers and she hesitated, stopped, restarted and then nearly flung the guitar on the floor.

"Fry it!" and she put the guitar down before she was tempted to break it.

She sat with her chin in her hands, puzzling over the music. Her anger was down to a simple fact: she wanted to get onto Lunar Tunes - a local talent show that had been arranged between the habitats across the Moon. The broadcasting services that were dedicated to lunar programming were hard pressed to find good material in a sterile and hostile environment so everything came back to programs about people. The Lunar Tunes franchise had been successful and this was the third series - and Melody was determined to live up to her name.

In her head, she gave herself a good talking to and, picking up the guitar again, she began the song once more. It was a cover of a song made popular back on Earth by the singer, Jacelynn Wales - a teenager not much older than Melody, when she recorded it. Its title was *I'm me. This is mine.* and it had hit the music charts the previous year.

Jacelynn's voice was similar to Melody's, but Melody managed to get more emotion into the song ... but the chords were defeating her. Time and again, she sang and played and time and again stumbled over the same chord sequence. Eventually, she decided that enough was enough.

"I'm not going to get this today - I'll go see Xalata."

And so saying, she headed to the door of the home, let herself out and pressed the alert button next to Xalata's home.

"Hey Melody," said Xalata, "what's happening?"

"Same old," said Melody. "I'm going to break my guitar soon if I can't work out how to play that chord sequence."

Xalata had already experienced Melody's frustration but she genuinely believed that her friend's voice was good enough to win the competition.

"Here's a thought," she said, "why don't you just practice the chords but don't sing at the same time? Every time I've seen you do the song, you're always singing too. If you just keep repeating that section, it should come good, surely?"

"Yeah, maybe you're right," said Melody. "I can't go back to it now though. My finger ends have worn until they're sore from the guitar strings and to be honest, I don't have the patience today."

"Oh, what's the prob?"

"I dunno. I've done my Tri-v for Wiglet and I'm not sure I've really done what he wants. That's getting in the way. And, well to be honest, this whole thing with the Asttarians is getting my head."

"So, generally, you're in a panic?"

"Uh-huh. Fret by name..."

"And by nature too. Y'know, I've only known you a little while and you actually *do* fret about pretty much everything," laughed Xalata.

"Well, it's not easy being a Scaredy cat all the time - I just seem to be scared of my own shadow. Mum got me a break placement last year with a big company that has a facility in Habitat 22. I wouldn't go 'cos I didn't know anyone. Mum was furious."

Xalata wrinkled her nose. If Melody was feeling skippy about stuff, then how much more should Xalata be feeling that things were generally unstable - yet she didn't. She couldn't put her finger on why - perhaps it was that she'd always been her own person or maybe she just felt more confident, having had a fresh start, getting away from her history and generally beginning again.

"Look," she said, "I'm not sure it's any help, but the Asttarians thing is on the other side of the Moon from us. I think it should be the least of your worries. You can sing and play as well as anyone I know - you're just frying your wiring because you've not psyched yourself up for this."

Melody didn't look convinced. "Easy for you to say, but I'm the one going to be standing up in front of everyone and singing. It's like showing off your soul to people - and I'm scared!"

"Yeah, but remember that you can do this - I've heard you sing..."

"Not this song - I can't get the chords right."

"Another song, mebbe?"

"No, it has to be this one."

By now, Melody was getting a bit tearful.

"Sorry," said Xalata, "I'm putting pressure on you and that won't help. Anyway, why do you think your Tri-v isn't good enough?"

"I think it's OK - I just have this feeling that I missed the point."

At that moment, Xalata's pad buzzed quietly. "Who's this...?" and she opened it to see Glitch's face grinning at her.

"Hey, Xalata," he said, "I'm right near your home - fancy letting me in for a juice?"

"What," said Xalata, "are you mad? My dad would spit feathers if he knew I'd invited someone into the home. Sorry, friend. Another day perhaps - catch ya!"

"Wait, wait!" said Glitch, just as Xalata was about to dim the pad. "Don't you want to know why I stopped by?"

"Why did you stop by, Glitch?" said Xalata.

"Let me in and I'll tell you..."

"Bye Glitch..."

"No, no, OK. Erm ... I wanted to invite you to a seminar..."

"What?"

"Yeah, a seminar at the Outpost at Central Air Facility. I know you're keen on the plant biology bit of our course and there's a woman giving a seminar. Her name's Castrana Machin - she's top dollar on the subject and she's visiting the Facility. My folks are going and I thought of you. Wanna come too?"

"Hmm. Maybe," said Xalata. "Come in - I'll buzz the door."

She pressed a space on her pad and moments later, Glitch walked into the room. He looked nervous - uncomfortable really and not at all like his usual bouncy, annoying self.

"So, um, what do you say? You gonna come with me?" He fiddled with his fingers and glanced uneasily around the room.

"Glitch, sit down and take a chill pill, for Frank's sake." Melody piped up from the other side of the room.

"Oh, hi Melody. Sorry - didn't know you were here too. I, um ... there's only one spare ticket so, um I can't..."

"No problem, don't sweat - I probably can't go anyway. My Mum is not letting me go out alone because of the Asttarian thing..."

"Hey, great ... I mean, sure, OK."

"Glitch," said Xalata, "when, where?"

"Oh, right. Yeah, it's tomorrow at 2pm - no classes tomorrow afternoon so we can get the *exeat* and go off to the event. It's at the Outpost."

"Don't know the Outpost - what's that?"

"It's a sort of conference place, right near the spaceport where you landed. So you'll know it anyway. We could go together if you like?"

"Oh, how romantic," giggled Melody.

"Give over, Melody," said Xalata, "this better not be some sort of thing to hit on me, Glitch."

"No, really," he protested, "my folks will be there too, when we get to the event. Honest, I wouldn't do that..."

"No? Mr Freeze? Why don't I believe you?"

"Look," said Glitch, "it's straight up. Really. You've got to come with me."

"Got to? Why?"

"Sorry, no that's not what I meant. I mean, it would be great if you came too and I think you'll like the event."

Xalata sighed, looked at Melody, looked back to Glitch.

"OK - I'll come - just need to check with Dad."

"Sure - no problem. I need to go now..."

And with that, Glitch scuttled towards the door.

Chapter Eleven

"And that concludes my Tri-v!" Melody had just shown her Tri-v to Wiglet and a few of the others in her year had joined her to see what she had done.

"Most commendable, Melody. I think you have summed up the task very well. Your method and processes were logical and your conclusions were excellent. That was quite a 'textbook' Tri-v and I'd like you to share it with the others."

"Really?" said Melody, the relief very evident on her face. "Gosh, I'm so pleased, Mr Wiggins. I was not certain I had picked up the right idea, but once I was on it, I followed it through to the end. Thank you so much."

She beamed with delight and the others in the group shared her pleasure in the achievement - apart from Bad Penny who, as usual, had turned up late and was glowering at the back of the room. Her alter ego, Rose Pretty, had also arrived a little late, just before Penny. She smiled, the way a cat smiles before it pounces on a mouse.

"Wonderful, Melody dahling. You must be so proud!" She tipped her head to one side and bared her teeth at Melody, just at an angle where Wiglet couldn't see. "So delighted that we can all share in your expertise."

"Er, thanks, Rose. I, er..."

"Oh look, the poor lamb is lost for words," she said to no one in particular. Then she swung back to Melody and hissed, "You need to back off, you pushy little tart. Keep out of my face."

Xalata was prepping her own Tri-v at the other side of the room and saw Rose's attitude to Melody.

"Hey, Pretty Thing. Leave my friend alone!"

"Or? Newbie Earthling? What's your big secret? What can you do, huh? Leap off the edge, loser." And she walked slowly to the back of the room.

Not wanting to get drawn into an exchange, but pleased to see that Rose and Penny had now moved away, she said to Melody,

"They're bullies. Just stand up to them. You don't need to be afraid of them - what are they going to do? It's all words - and if they make it physical, there are loads of witnesses."

"I'm not as brave as you..."

"I'm not brave," said Xalata, "I just don't want to be pushed about by two good-for-nothings like them."

The group was gathering again, as it was time for Xalata's Tri-v.

"Hard act to follow, Fret!" she grinned at Melody. Melody smiled back and sat herself down, ready for Xalata's presentation.

"OK Miss Orbit, would you like to present please?" said Wiglet, turning to the rest of the group and indicating that they should sit down and pay attention.

"Sure, thanks Mr Wiggins. I've rather done my Tri-v a different way, if you're OK with that. I thought that I would make the Tri-v more vivid. My topic is hybridisation in the aquacultures - something I've been looking at in depth. And I'm going to a lecture this afternoon about it..."

"Castrana Machin? That lecture? I would have liked to have gone to that myself," said Wiglet.

"Yes, that's the one. Anyway, here's my Tri-v," and the giant display vector appeared in front of the group.

The presentation was made of vivid movies, 3D and colourful with demonstrations of the points that Xalata was making, tied together with short pieces of narration, voiced by Xalata and backed by a simple yet effective soundtrack of music. The most impressive bits were when plant growth was shown in time-lapse and then dissolved into plant-based graphs and charts.

The group of students watched as the images unfolded, blended and morphed into dynamic shapes that made her points very clearly.

As the Tri-v drew to a close, there was a stunned silence in the room. It was broken by Rose, predictably.

"My, my. The Earthling learned animation back in the swamp."

"Why, thank you Rose for such a typically sweet and generous compliment," said Xalata, flashing her eyes at Rose to indicate that she need not carry on the exchange.

"Well, we have had two remarkable presentations today, I must say." Wiglet was not quite certain what to make of Xalata's. "Most unconventional, Xalata and quite effective. I'm not sure how the Board of Assessors would look on that, but nonetheless, no one can deny that you have put in a significant amount of work here."

"Thanks, Mr Wiggins," said Xalata and she sat down with the others as the display disappeared.

Several of the students moved over to speak to her and to Melody. But their minds were elsewhere. Xalata was concerned that she had not been able to speak to her Dad about the event with Glitch. She was having second thoughts about the seminar that afternoon, but now she had spilled the fact that she was going, there was no turning back.

Meanwhile, Melody was still anxious about the bullying comments made by Rose. *I wish I could just stand up to her, but I daren't,* she thought. *I so hate being this soft!*

Xalata had noticed that Glitch had steered out of her way all morning - *Strange, if he's invited me to the presentation,* she mused.

"Hey, Glitch. Don't like me any more?"

"Oh, hi Xalata. Sorry, I was just busy catching up. My Tri-v is next week so I was, er, sort of getting some pointers from you and Melody. You still OK for this afternoon?"

"Yep - wouldn't miss it for the world. I'll meet you at the TransTrak - what time do we need to leave?"

"Um, I think just after we've had our snack. That good for you?"

"Sure. See you there."

She still couldn't get a handle on why he was so nervous but she put it down to him just being a boy and therefore normally a bit odd. She flipped open her pad to look at her latest assignments when the news feed caught her eye: "*Lunar habitat closed off after attack.*"

The article showed some handheld video of the interior of Habitat 14 - the area that had been badly damaged by the Cryomorph. Huge holes gaped in the walls of the habitat, exposing the spaces behind but also evidently exposing the area to the full vacuum of space - impossible for anyone to operate here without the proper space suit and helmet. The narration gave more details:

Since the attack on Habitat 14 - part of the Farside lunar complex - assessors have been trying to establish how badly damaged the area is. During their last visit, they completely closed off all access to the site and have declared it uninhabitable. Facilities teams from LunarBase have been preparing to program the nano-constructors to repair the area, but the damage is such that there are serious problems in access and in repairing the structure.

"Wow," said Melody, who had just appeared at Xalata's shoulder, "That's really going to mess up the development program on Farside."

"Development program? What program?" said Xalata.

"The Research and Development department of your Dad's unit has been exploring some new techniques for terraforming - I think it's part of the Mars program. They want to make Mars have a breathable atmosphere and so a lot of it is down to plant biology, I think. Anyway, I don't know the details because they're secret, but I think that's why the Asttarians are attacking Habitat 14 - that's where the work is meant to start happening in a few months."

"OK - that explains why Dad wasn't home last night," said Xalata. *I guess I'll just have to go to the lecture without telling him.* "I'll see you later, Melody. I'm off to get something to eat then I'm meeting Glitch. Can you take my pad with you - I don't think I'll need it this afternoon."

"Sure," said Melody and smiled as Xalata headed for the door and waved to Glitch. As Melody turned away, she didn't see the look of panic on his face.

The Coming Threat

Hurtling through space, the giant rock rotated with the pressure from the fusion engines. In the far distance, a tiny glow in the blackness of space - The Earth - where control engineers have yet to discover two things: the rock is approaching on a trajectory that would mean it could impact the Earth; the second, that they no longer have any control of the huge and potentially devastating weapon that someone is pointing towards the Home Planet.

Second by second, minute by minute, the massive chunk of space debris moves closer to its new target and further away from the original target of Mars. And, silently, a hand moves the controls in a bunker deep under the Moon's surface and the route to Earth's destruction is finalised.

Chapter Twelve

The TransTrak was busy with excited people heading for the lecture at The Outpost. Glitch, true to his word, had turned up and now seemed a bit more relaxed as the speeding vehicle headed through the tunnels back to the Central Air Facility headquarters.

"So, what was up with you earlier today, Glitch?" said Xalata, her eyes searching his face for signs of the previous unease.

"Me? Nothing? As I said, I'm just concentrating on my Tri-v."

"Just that you looked anxious - as if you had something on your mind..."

Glitch laughed, "Nah, not me. Cool as a 'berg, me."

Xalata was not convinced, but she decided to drop the subject and, anyway, the TransTrak was slowing down, ready to dock in the station. "OK, nearly there. Do you have the passes to get us in?"

"Sure," replied Glitch. "They're right here on my pad. The entry will identify us automatically."

Sure enough, after they'd got off the train and headed the short distance to the Outpost, the gates opened and admitted them both to the auditorium. It wasn't as big as Xalata had expected but then, nothing much on The Moon was. The difficulties of providing a secure environment, protected from the Moon's hostile vacuum, complete with gravity, over a large space was a challenge even for the advanced engineering that made up the entire LunarBase.

As they walked into the room and found their seats, they saw an imperious-looking woman with a mane of silvery hair, standing talking to a group at the front of the stage. She was tall and elegant with a slightly hooked nose and she wore a robe - unusual for people on the Moon - which shimmered with reflected light on tiny black panels that covered its surface.

"That's Castrana Machin," whispered Glitch.

"Yeah, I guessed," replied Xalata, trying to get a better look at the renowned space biologist. "She looks a bit scary."

"My mum's met her, I think. She's supposed to be really clever but a bit odd. I suppose, we shall see what she's like soon."

The auditorium continued to fill but there was no sign of Glitch's parents or, if they were there, they must have been seated in another part of the room. Only a few minutes later, the lights dimmed, a man whom Xalata did not know, stood and introduced her and then Castrana Machin strode onto the stage to some polite applause.

"Ladies and gentlemen, academics and students, thank you for coming to hear what I have to say today. I am in two minds about how I feel, speaking to a meeting here on the Moon. We live in exciting and dangerous times. Threats from the very environment in which we live are overwhelming us and we live in a state of fear."

There were some shuffles from the audience and a couple of puzzled glances around the room.

"My talk today confronts those challenges, awakens a new hope in humankind and pushes the boundaries of where we are today, back to where they should be. We have sinned. We have ignored the warnings of the world around us. We have become arrogant as if we were the Lords of Creation themselves. We are not. We are but ants that scuttle across the surface of the Earth, its moon and soon, on to Mars. Beyond there, who knows?"

There was now a definite air of unease in the room and several people muttered to each other, as it was evident that the speaker was not going to stick to the topic of her talk.

"The Gods do not accept lightly the blasphemy that is being uttered every time we step outside our preordained limits. The biology that serves us is the very fabric of our being and yet we abuse it, stretch it, batter it into submission.

"Mankind will learn very soon that this can go on no longer. A vengeance is coming, a terrible and mighty vengeance..."

At this point one of the audience stood up and interjected, "Excuse me Ms Machin, but this appears to be a significant diversion away from the theme of hybridisation..."

"Yes," she replied, "because the times are upon us and it is too late for talk. Action is the only thing that will save us." Her voice boomed around the auditorium and she stood with a strange gleam in her eye that made her look even more unearthly than she had before. She seemed to fix every person in the room with her stare and Xalata simply stared back as the piercing gaze swept the auditorium.

Suddenly, her face relaxed into a half-smile. Her voice became quieter, softer and she said, "There's a Way of life that's right and another that's wrong. If you don't keep to the Way, bad things happen. I'll say no more, but you'll find out soon enough."

And with that, she swept off the stage, officials from the Outpost scurrying after her. The audience erupted into a burst of chatter as each person turned to others next to them to exclaim about the strange and very brief appearance of Castrana Machin.

"Wow, that was weird," said Xalata. "What was she on about? She sounded like those Asttarian nuts for a moment there."

"Frank knows," said Glitch, "but I'm certain that we'll hear more about it soon. We were supposed to go and meet her after the talk. Do you think she'll be there? We could ask her what she meant."

"Really? You want to go into the same room as that nutter? Her circuits are well fried. Count me out, I'm going..."

"Aw, c'mon, where's your sense of adventure? Let's go find her."

The room was clearing now and Xalata looked in the direction that Glitch was pointing. "I think it's down there - at least, that's the way she went out," she said.

Always one for a challenge she led the way and headed towards the door behind the stage. As they pushed the door open, the corridor beyond looked quite dark, but they could hear voices raised in the distance.

"Someone's not happy about that speech," said Xalata as they shuffled forward into the gloom.

They slowly moved toward the sound of the argument and then, suddenly and soundlessly, a strong pair of arms came out of the darkness and grabbed Xalata. One hand went over her mouth and the other held her tight as she struggled and kicked. She tried to shout out, but she could only make a muffled noise.

As she felt another pair of hands take hold of her legs she realized she was going to be dragged bodily out of the corridor and into an adjacent room. She kicked as hard as she could and felt a foot connect with flesh. There was a muffled "Oomph" as her attacker struggled to get their wind back.

She looked wildly around. The attacker in front of her was dressed completely in black including a black mask covering the entire head. Only the eyes showed through and they looked angry. The person in front pulled back a fist as if to strike, but the one holding her stopped the punch. "No, she's not to be hurt."

She looked back into the corridor as she was hauled into the side room and saw Glitch, just standing there, tears in his eyes. He gulped and said as the door closed, "I'm so sorry..."

Chapter Thirteen

Back at the Academy, Melody was attending to some of her coursework when Glitch walked in, looking very shaken.

"Where's Xalata? Didn't she come back with you?"

"No," replied Glitch, "she just went off on her own after the talk and I couldn't find her. The talk was weird and I think Xalata wanted to talk to Castrana Machin to discover what the freak she was on about."

"Weird? What do you mean?" said Melody, with a hint of suspicion in her voice.

"She was talking about "the Gods" and "the times are upon us" and all sorts of bizarre stuff that didn't make much sense."

"So she didn't give a talk on biology then?"

"Nope - it lasted about two minutes and that was it. Xalata went after her when she left the auditorium. I was just chatting to someone else and when I looked round, Xalata had disappeared."

"So did you try to find her?"

"I couldn't - security weren't letting anyone through so, I thought she'd probably find her own way back."

Melody looked sceptical, but she nodded and said, "OK - we'll just have to wait for her. I can't go back to the home without her. What would her Dad say? In fact, did he know she was going?"

"Dunno. I expect she'll go straight back home though. Probably best to wait for her there?"

She gathered her things together and headed for the door. "She's from Earth you know, Glitch. It was your duty to look after her and I think you've let her down. I just hope for your sake that she turns up."

Glitch shuffled his feet and looked uncomfortable. "I couldn't do anything, honest. She just upped and went and by the time I realized, she'd gone."

Melody gave him a glance and then walked out of the door to head back to the home. She was worried - Glitch should have stayed with Xalata. Why had he let her go? She could be anywhere. She headed for the TransTrak.

*   *   *   *   *   *

Back at the home, there was no sign of Xalata. Nor could Melody raise her on messaging. In fact, it was as if she had disappeared completely. When Brett arrived home that evening, Melody went straight to his home and told the story.

"Why did no one tell me she was missing? Why didn't you tell Adolf?" said Brett. "I don't understand how she can have been there one moment and then gone the next."

"We thought she would turn up, Mr Orbit - I'm really sorry. I know I should have told you or Mr Fark, but Glitch seemed certain that there was no reason to worry."

"Right, we need to get things moving. I'm going to speak to Adolf and then I'll get over to The Outpost to search for her."

"I'll come too..."

"No, you stay here in case she returns. Just let me know if you hear anything," and, with that Brett hurried out of the door, his communicator to his ear as he went.

Melody sat down in the Orbit's home and looked around. There was nothing she could do. It was pointless waiting. If Xalata came back then all was fine, but why would she when she'd been missing for a couple of hours now? Maybe she'd got into conversation with Castrana Machin and had forgotten the time? The truth was, no one knew and time was moving on.

Suddenly, she decided. *I'm going to go and look for her. But I'm taking Mr Shaw-Storey with me ... or should that be Mr Tall-Story?* she mused. She was not at all convinced by Glitch's explanation and she knew that something was wrong ... therefore, she needed to find her friend.

Picking up her pad, she buzzed Glitch, told him what was happening and, over-riding his protests, strode out of the home and headed for the TransTrak.

*   *   *   *   *   *

Glitch met her at the station platform, "Look, is this a good idea? Shouldn't you wait back at the home in case she arrives? Where do you think we are going to look?"

"I don't know and I don't care. She's my friend and I'm going to try and find her, after *you* lost her! I don't know what you're not telling me, Glitch, but when I find out, you're gonna be in big trouble. Now, get yourself on that train and let's find her."

The TransTrak pulled out of the station and headed at speed into the tunnel. Glitch stood with his eyes lowered, studying his boots while Melody tried to contact Xalata again across The Q, on her pad. There was no response and she put it into her bag. As the train hurtled through the tunnels, back to the LunarBase, she decided that she would follow Xalata's tracks as far as she could, with the help of Glitch - or not.

The train slowed to a standstill and they both stepped out onto the platform. It was quiet now, as most people had gone back to their homes, so they made good progress down the ramp towards the Outpost. When they arrived, they found that the doors were closed but a security guard was seated at a desk inside. Melody rattled the door and the guard looked up and waved his head, mouthing, "We're closed."

Melody shouted through the glass, "It's urgent. I left my pad here when I was at today's lecture. Can I come and look for it?"

The guard came over to the door and said, "We've had no pads handed in."

"Oh, I think I may have put it under my seat..."

"Crazy thing to do. We're still closed."

"Look, it's urgent, I need it for my course. I'm at the Hydroponics Department at the Academy. If I don't get my pad, I can't do my Tri-v tomorrow and I'll be in such trouble..." she ended with a sob and real tears appeared at the corner of her eyes.

"It's more than me job's worth, young lady..."

"Oh please! Help me..." and she broke down crying. Glitch put an arm around her as if to comfort her.

"I don't think he's going for it, Melody," he whispered. "We ought to go back."

"Shut up, idiot," Melody hissed and renewed her howling.

At that moment, the guard opened the door. "OK, but you need to be quick. If anyone finds out, I'm for it. Now get a move on." And he pushed them both through the door and pointed out the auditorium. "The lights are on in there now. Be back here in five minutes."

Melody and Glitch hurried to the door. "Where did that all come from," said Glitch. "Why are you so upset?"

"You really don't get it do you? I'm a girl. Girls can cry. On demand. Now, move it!"

Glitch looked puzzled and worried but followed Melody into the auditorium. "Right," she said, "show me where you went and where you sat." Glitch led the way and pointed out the seats. Melody hurried over to them and then called across to him, "And where did she go when she disappeared?"

He pointed to the door next to the podium. "So why didn't you follow her?"

"Er, I don't know. I was talking to someone, as I said and I just saw her go through the door and then she had gone."

"So didn't you follow her?" said Melody, walking over to the door.

"I went and opened the door a few moments later but it was dark in there and, um, a security person came and told me I couldn't go in."

Melody pushed through the door into the dark corridor behind. "Here, hold this door open now so I get some light in. I can't find the light controls." She moved further in once Glitch had held the door and began to look for rooms off to the side.

Glitch called to her, "I think the guard is coming. We really ought to be getting out of here," then Melody caught sight of a glint of colour on the floor near a dark door. Just as she was about to move towards it she heard the voice of the guard:

""Ere, what are you doing in there. You was only supposed to be searching the auditorium." Glitch let go the door and the corridor was plunged into blackness, but Melody had already grabbed the item on the floor and pushed it into her bag. As she did so, the door opened once more and the guard, visibly angry, stood there. "What you think you're doing? Why have you come in 'ere?"

"Sorry, sir," said Melody, tearful once more. "I panicked - I thought that I might have gone out this way and dropped my pad. Then it went dark. Really sorry," and she hurried through the door and back into the auditorium. She and Glitch then made for the exit with the guard right behind them.

"I'll need to let you out, now be off with you. Bloomin' kids today. Give 'em a nanometre and they take a parsec."

With that, he pushed them without ceremony out of the door and locked it behind them.

"Phew!" said Glitch.

"Phew? Is that all you can say? Xalata is round here somewhere and you're relieved that you didn't get reported? You're a worm, *Justin*!" and she strode off back to the TransTrak.

Chapter Fourteen

Back at the home, Melody checked her bag. She hadn't wanted Glitch to see what she had found. Pulling out the object she saw that it was a brightly coloured titanium buckle - just like the ones that Xalata had on her boots (that she seemed never to take off). She'd been wearing those boots ever since she arrived; in fact, Melody reckoned that she didn't have any other footwear. Fortunately, they were OK for the requirements that LunarBase had for flooring surfaces in the habitats and public spaces so she had not had to change them.

Now though, Melody stared at the buckle and wondered aloud, "Where are you then? You went into the dark corridor and then something happened - something that meant your buckle came off." She turned it over and saw that the fixing on the back had snapped. It was made of metal too, like the rest of the buckle and was not meant to come off the boot. *Therefore,* thought Melody, *that's come off with force.*

She thought back to the dark doorway that she had seen, just where she had found the buckle and she realized that it was likely that it was through that door that Xalata had gone when she disappeared. "But where's the door go to?" she mused and then, clicking her brain into gear, she got out her pad and searched The Q for plans of the Outpost. They were not easy to find, but Melody was a resourceful girl and she did something that she had always said she would not do - used her Mum's access codes to get into more confidential areas of information. "I'll be fried for this," she muttered, but she kept on hunting.

The Outpost itself was a relatively new structure in the original LunarBase habitat so its details were in more recent plans that gave an overview of the whole base. Then, she found what she needed - a 3D visual plan and walkthrough of the habitat itself, with the various institutions, the Praesidium, the Academy and other important buildings clearly marked. This information was usually confidential, but with her Mum's access, Melody could see everything she needed.

Using the 3D visualization she walked through the entrance lobby where she had had her encounter with the guard and into the auditorium. Everything looked super-real and reflected the current appearance of the area. Although it did not include actual people, the signs of their presence were even marked on the plans, with visible details even down to the security screens on the guard's desk.

There was the podium and, to the left of it, the doorway into the back of the building. Moving herself through the simulation she passed through the doorway and headed to the area on the left where she had seen the dark door. The corridor appeared as it would if it was lit and so the doors and corridors were easy to spot, but there was no door at all where Melody had found the buckle. The wall was just continuous. "Yet, I saw it, so it must be there," she muttered again.

As she had spent a lot of her childhood alone, she had become very good at some types of online games and so she automatically treated the simulation as if she was in a game. *If the door's supposed to be there, then it must be there*, she thought to herself as she attempted to walk herself through the solid walls at the spot where the dark door had appeared. Still nothing. She tried once more and, at this point, a warning flashed on the screen:

NO ACCESS. YOUR CLEARANCE DOES NOT AUTHORISE YOU TO VIEW THIS AREA.

"Ha ha!" she exclaimed. "So there *is* something there." And she set about trying to find a work around to bypass the blockage. "If my Mum's access can't get through here, then I'll just have to try someone else's," and she logged out and keyed in another access, one that she had learned quite by accident, when she had seen Wiglet logging into his portal.

She found the plans once more and dived into the simulation, this time as one Waldorf Wiggins. *Waldorf?* she thought. *Ouch. Someone was unkind.*

The Outpost swung into view in clear three dimensions and she once again passed through the lobby and auditorium, into the dark corridor. With Wiglet's access, the door was there, quite clearly and, with her heart in her mouth, she moved herself forward through it into the space beyond. As she gasped with shock at what she saw, the visualization disappeared from view and an alert box flashed on the screen:

ACCESS VIOLATION! ILLEGAL ACCESS. SECURITY RESPONSE INITIATED.

Chapter Fifteen

Melody stood in shock in front of her pad, the flashing sign giving her clear news that her pad was locked down and inaccessible. What she had seen had left her speechless, but now she realized the significance of it and hurried out of the door to her home, stopping only to grab Xalata's pad, which her friend had left with her as she departed for the Outpost.

She crossed the small atrium that led back into the various homes in this cluster and headed down a side tunnel that would lead her around the back of the main access route. As she ran, she heard the sound of feet in the other tunnels and, looking back, she saw Adolf Fark and a group of armed security men running up the access-way to her home. She pulled back against the wall of the tunnel as they dashed past and then, without wasting a moment, hurried off, getting herself as far away from the scene as possible.

But where to go? She couldn't go back to the Academy - Wiglet would certainly know that she had "borrowed" his access. If she went to find her mother, she would get the most dreadful strip torn off her. And she couldn't go back home, for obvious reasons. The girl called Fret started to do just that.

"Get a grip, for Frank's sake," she muttered to herself, "you've only yourself to blame so either face the music or go and find Xalata. Brave enough are we?" She often taunted herself to try and kick herself into action when she was in tricky situations, but this one beat all the scrapes she had been in before and she felt very alone and scared.

What she had seen in the secret room, through the 3D visualisation, was the spur that got her going. As the door had opened, the view in front of her was of a strange and desolate habitat, totally unlike the one that she lived in. The walls were even more plain, if that was possible and there was a feeling of isolation about the place that was confirmed when she saw the navigation prompt at the bottom of the screen: "Habitat 14". Little-used tunnels led off from the access point where she stood and there was no sign of anyone living there.

From everything that she had seen on the newsfeed, Habitat 14 had been where the Cryomorph destruction had taken place ... and it was on Farside. Therefore, somehow, unlikely though it seemed, this doorway that she had been visualised for her was a portal through space, and perhaps even through time, to a location on the other side of the Moon.

"And if that's where that door leads, then Xalata went there. And it's where I have to go now, to find her." She gulped at the thought of what she had to do, but once again she teased herself and persuaded her subconscious that, yes, this would be a great idea. Her conscious mind was violently disagreeing, needless to say.

She set off, looking over her shoulder and headed for the TransTrak. She had no idea how she was going to get to Habitat 14, but the answer had to lie in the Outpost and its secret doorway.

*   *   *   *   *   *

It was quite late in the day when Melody arrived at the Outpost. It was busy there and she had successfully avoided the security people who were quite evidently looking for her. She knew though that it was only a matter of time before she was spotted on a ViewCam. Her best bet was that the level of security alert had not been raised, so that her disappearance would only be a small issue.

Hoping against hope, she walked past the Outlook and checked out the situation. There was an evening event just beginning - a concert, by the looks of the formal dress that people were wearing as they arrived. There was no chance of getting inside by the main entrance because she had no virtual ticket for a seat, so she was just going to have to be inventive.

Moving around the outside perimeter, she spotted a smaller door that was evidently the Stage Door as a number of musicians were walking in. She screwed up her courage to screaming point and simply joined the group of young people who were heading for the interior of the Outpost.

"Dressing rooms are on the left down corridor 3," said a guard to the group as they walked by. No request for ID or access - she was in. She followed the group further down the corridor and then, at the first opportunity, peeled off into a small side room that seemed to be unused. The problem was that she had no idea where she was in the building, although she was fairly certain she was at least on the correct side, near the dark corridor.

She determined that she would wait until the concert started and then prowl the area backstage until she found the right corridor. She dug around in her bag and found an energy bar and then settled down to wait. Outside, she could hear more people passing and she prayed that she would not be disturbed so that she could continue the hunt for Xalata.

Chapter Sixteen

So, here she was, trapped in a home on Farside. Why, she had no idea. By whom? Likewise. All she knew was that, once she had been captured, she had been bundled up, dumped on a vehicle and then driven to who knows where.

Mysterious threats if she didn't behave had terrified her. Even more strange was the fact that the place had been prepared for her - there were clothes in the bedroom for her age and size and a fridge full of meals.

Xalata quickly realized that there was not much that she could do. She was locked in and powerless and there seemed to be no way to get in touch with anyone she knew. Worse still, she had no idea where she was and couldn't recall anything much that would give her a clue ...other than the strange sight of the derelict looking environment that had met her eyes, just as the bag went on her head.

Why's there a place like that on LunarBase? she mused. Everything was always clean and well kept whereas this place had seemed almost abandoned. Yet the home she was sitting in now was in good condition and had obviously been maintained. *I don't get it.*

She went back to the airlock door and hammered on it, shouting, "Anybody out there?" There was silence so she hammered some more, "Get me out of here!" She thought she heard a small sound outside the door, but they were usually very soundproof so it may have been her imagination. Once more, she hammered, "Open this freakin' door!"

Then, there suddenly was a sound - a voice reverberated around the lobby where she was standing, "Be quiet! If you won't be quiet, then we shall have to take steps to make you quiet. Now be a good girl, my dear. Sit down. Have something to eat. Watch a movie. You'll be here for a while."

The voice finished - it had been the same guy as had captured her - *my dear,* again - and he obviously had a sound feed into the rooms of the home. He was probably watching her too, she thought and she glanced around, looking for the telltale signs of small lenses, picking up her movements. No sign, but that didn't mean they weren't there.

She walked back to the living space and flopped down on a chair. There was nothing for her to do. No sooner had she sat though, than she heard movement in the lobby and the door to the living space opened to reveal two people - one smaller and the other taller. Both were masked and wore uniformly black clothing.

"Stay where you are," the taller person said. "Here's more food for your fridge. You will stay here and you'll keep quiet - no one is around to hear you. This place is deserted, but we don't want to disturb...", he or, in fact possibly she, paused. "We don't want to be disturbed by you as we have important work to do."

Xalata couldn't recognize the voice - it was either a light man's voice or a quite deep woman's. The clothing hid their body shapes so she really couldn't tell one way or another. The smaller person went to the refrigerator, opened the door and slid inside some parcels of food that had been carried in a black bag. The fridge door closed and the two people then moved out of the room backwards, watching Xalata for any sudden movement.

What had the taller person been about to say - *We don't want to disturb ...* what? Xalata sat and thought back. What had the guy said when she had been captured and the bag was being pulled over her head? *We don't want to wake the bogeyman now do we?*

The Hammer of Asttar

It moves with unstoppable power. As big as a city block and, with the destructive power of many thousands of nuclear weapons, it hurtles towards Earth at thousands of miles per hour - a speed that will ensure that the destruction caused by its impact will be far-reaching, utterly wiping out the area around the target zone and throwing Earth into a "nuclear winter" from which it will not emerge for many years.

The controlling hands on the Moon fine tune the override on the navigation and boost the engines to provide even more speed.

The clock is ticking. Earth has only four days left.

Chapter Eighteen

The small room was stuffy and dark and Melody was constantly in fear that someone would open the door and discover her. The concert had obviously not yet begun, because there were still people moving about outside and the noises from the auditorium came faintly through the door. She had been in this confined space for nearly half an hour and her courage was beginning to fail her. *What am I doing here? I must be mad! When Wiglet discovers I have used his ID to get access to the top-level areas, there'll be hell to pay.*

Yet her fears were drowned out by thoughts of her new friend Xalata and the fact that something - she didn't yet know what - had happened to her and she had disappeared. With that in her mind she screwed up her courage and cajoled herself to do what had to be done.

As she thought about it, there were some louder noises from outside the door - the sound of a number of people coming up the corridor towards her hiding place. Probably they were going out of the exit that was nearby, past the guard. As she listened the footsteps came closer and then, horror, they stopped outside the door.

"I'll see you back in the auditorium, Scott," said a voice, seeming almost next to her ear, "I just need to get some cleaning things to mop up the mess that Penny has made with the food."

Penny! Bad Penny? Was she here - and who was it speaking? With a jolt she realized that the speaker was Rose Pretty and that, worse still, she was headed in through that very door. Melody grabbed the door handle with the idea of holding tight so that Rose couldn't pull open the door. As she did so, her finger caught on a small latch, just below the handle.

"See you later then," came a man's voice and Melody felt a pressure on the handle as Penny tried to turn it to get into the room. She fumbled with the handle, pulled with all her might and, with her free hand, flipped the latch next to the handle. Rose, on the outside tried to turn it, but of course, it was locked. She rattled the door and twisted the handle back and forth but nothing moved. Rose swore quietly under her breath and then moved off, back down the way she had come.

Melody, meanwhile, flopped back against the door, sweat from panic on her face and her heart pounding with adrenalin. *What's Rose doing here? She's not musical. And worse still, what's Penny here for?*

As if in answer to her question, footsteps came up the corridor again and the sound of two voices arguing:

"Of course I haven't seen 'er, I bin lookin' and there's no sign." Definitely Penny.

"You stupid idiot, she must be here somewhere - Scott saw her come in with the band. You need to look harder. I've no time for this - I have to be in the audience."

"Oh yeah, so everyone can look at you. Bloomin' lightweight. You wouldn't know how to look for an ice cube in a fridge - and don't go callin' me stupid. I'm as bright as you. I want that reward as much as you do..." Their voices faded into the distance.

Reward? Melody's ears pricked up. A reward? For her? Suddenly there was the sound of music wafting through the door and she realized that the concert had started and now was her chance to make her way behind the stage and find the doorway. With a good deal of trepidation, she unlocked the latch and turned the handle slowly, not wanting to make any noise in case there was someone still in the corridor. The last thing she wanted was to be caught by Penny and Rose!

With a quick look each way, she eased out into the deserted passageway and headed away from the direction she had come in. There didn't seem to be anyone around but she crept along silently, pausing at corners to peek around and check that the coast was clear. Peering round one corner a couple of moments later she realized that she was next to the entrance that led onto the stage. Through the door she could make out people standing in the wings, watching the performance and, beyond them were the musicians who were playing their hearts out. She couldn't see the audience, but sensed that the auditorium was full by the way that the sound didn't echo.

Now she had her bearings because this door was to the side of the stage and therefore it was the same one that Xalata must have come through when she was about to be captured. Melody felt a thrill of excitement - or was it fear? She stepped forward and, as she did so, a hand fell upon her shoulder. She almost screamed and turned to see a guard looking at her: "Where are you going, Miss? The concert's in there and your colleagues are all in place."

"Oh, sorry, yes. I, erm." She felt herself flush with fear. She suppressed it quickly. "I look after the music scores. I'm just going to key up the pages for the second half so that everyone has it on their pads. The master one is in the Green Room." *Where did that come from?*

"OK, Miss. You know your way?"

"Sure, er yes. Thanks for your help, sir." And with that she took off around the back of the stage towards the area where she felt certain Xalata had been captured. *Phew! This is obviously the right direction for the Green Room or he would have come after me. I just need my luck to hold!*

As she moved further back behind the stage, the darkness hid the features of the area ahead of her. All lights were suppressed during a performance so there was no distracting light filtering onto the stage. Off to her right, light was coming through a gap made by a door that was ajar - probably the Green Room. However, off to her left she couldn't see a thing and that was where she needed to go. She sneaked over to the Green Room and pushed the door gently to open it wider, in case there were other people still remaining. All clear! With more light coming into the area she could now see a doorway that was in about the right position for the one she had discovered on the plans.

Taking the opportunity that there was still no one around, she darted over to the door and opened it. Nothing inside at all. It was completely empty and blank black walls looked back at her from what was ultimately a small, vacant cupboard. *OK. Why would you have an empty cupboard in a place like this? Surely it would be used for something. Therefore, it's not a cupboard, I believe.*

She stepped into the cupboard and pulled the door to, behind her. It was inky black now, but it had been no better when the door was open so she might as well have the protection of the door in case anyone passed by. Using her hands instead of her eyes, she felt around the walls and the doorframe, trying to locate something that would give her access to the space that she knew lay beyond. She tapped on the back wall, but it sounded absolutely solid to her knocking - no sign of secret panels or doors.

She could just reach the ceiling with her hands if she stood on tiptoe and she worked her way around the edge and then across it into the middle, scanning every square inch of space by touch alone. Still nothing, so she started on the door wall, working her way around the frame. It didn't seem a very logical place for a panel or a control, but nothing about this venture made much sense in any case.

As she worked her hands around the frame of the door, she felt an irregularity in the otherwise totally smooth wall, just to the left of the doorframe and near the floor. There appeared to be some sort of panel there, perhaps made of glass? She knelt down and passed her hand across the surface. As she did so, the panel glowed blue-white and an ID screen appeared. She knew what to do - without a moment's hesitation, she typed on the upside-down virtual keyboard (she wouldn't have been able to read it the right way up), Wiglet's access and password.

There was a moment's hesitation and then the back of the cupboard appeared to dissolve and the world went very bright indeed.

Chapter Nineteen

"You did WHAT?"

Brett towered over Glitch, who cowered back against the door. He had come to see Brett after realizing that his actions might have cost Xalata her life.

"I asked her to the lecture at The Outpost and ..."

"What, to see that charlatan, Castrana Machin? You must be insane. Her views on bio-sciences are extreme and she's a danger to young minds."

"Yes, but ..." Glitch tried to interject. "That's not the whole story, Mr Orbit sir. You see, the lecture ended early - but I knew it would - and ..."

"How could you possibly know that would happen ..."

"Please sir, let me finish. The lecture ended early and so I asked Xalata to go around the back of the auditorium, where Mrs Machin had gone, so that she could talk to her. I'd been told that I had to do that so that Xalata would come quietly."

"Whatever do you mean? Where's Xalata now?"

"Just coming to that bit, sir. We went around the back and it was very dark, but I'd been told to go to a specific door and wait with her there. So we did that and suddenly, Xalata was grabbed and pulled into the room behind the door. Except it didn't look like a room. I didn't know what to do. She was shouting and kicking, but the door suddenly slammed shut and I couldn't open it again."

"Who asked you to do this? Where are they and where's Xalata?"

"Really, I don't know Mr Orbit, sir. I'm really sorry, but they threatened me if I didn't do it ..."

"Who? Who threatened you?"

"Well ... I don't know, you see, I received messages on my pad that said my younger sister, Florence, is being held captive back on Earth. If I didn't do what they said then they'd hurt her.

"And you believed them?

"Well, yes. There was a clip of Flo tied to a chair and she was obviously a captive."

"And you believe this to be real?"

"Erm, yes, well, I hadn't really thought about it, but now you say, I suppose it could have been RealLife animation. That hadn't crossed my mind ..."

"Right," Brett picked up his pad and contacted Fark, "we'll deal with you later. The first priority is to find Xally and get her back. You'll need to take me to where you left her. You'd better ..." Fark responded on the pad. "Ah Adolf, we have a situation ..."

＊　　　＊　　　＊　　　＊　　　＊

After a delay of about twenty minutes while Fark arrived, they set off and about another twenty minutes later, Glitch, Brett and Fark arrived at The Outpost. The journey on the TransTrak had been tense and silent. Brett was anxious and angry. Fark was calm but edgy, while Glitch simply stood by the door and worried about what had happened to Xalata.

The concert was still playing when they arrived and the sound of the music greeted them as they walked into the building. The security guards immediately rose to their feet. "Sorry gentlemen, but you can't go in. The concert is ..."

"My daughter has been abducted," said Brett, "and I need to get around the back of the auditorium right now."

"Really sorry sir, but no unauthorised people are allowed back ..."

"I'll take care of this, Brett," said Fark. "Now listen to me, I am head of security at the Academy for Hydroponics and I have a hot line, direct to your boss. We are going backstage and nothing you can do will stop us. Not if you value your job, that is. Do I make myself clear, my man?" and he flashed his security credentials.

"Er, yes sir. I suppose so. I'll need to accompany you though."

"That's not necessary. I shall take full responsibility. Now, let us pass." And with that Fark strode round the barrier and headed to the doors that led backstage. Brett and Glitch came along quickly behind him. The corridor was dark once again.

"It was like this when we were here earlier," said Glitch. "You could hardly see where you were going."

"Then you had better have a good memory for dark environments," said Fark, as they made their way further behind the performance on stage.

"I think it's here," said Glitch, pointing to a door on the left, set back from the corridor. "It was difficult to see when we were here, but this is the one, I'm sure."

"OK," said Brett, "Let's get inside and see what's happening." They turned the handle and revealed a simple, empty cupboard.

"That's not how it looked when Xalata was pulled through," said Glitch. "There was light and I could see into the distance. There must be a panel in there that opens somehow."

Fark stepped into the cupboard and made a great performance of tapping, pushing and listening. "There's absolutely nothing here, Justin. Nothing. I think you are either making up a story to put us off the track or you have brought us to the wrong place, either deliberately or accidentally. Either way, we are not making progress. Think again please."

"I just don't know, Mr Fark. I'm really sorry. I'm sure it was this door. There's not another one along here that I can see and we were definitely down this corridor ..."

"Then, I think you had better come with me and we will see what is to be done with you." And with that, Fark strode out of the cupboard and headed back to the main entrance. Brett and Glitch both took a look into the cupboard but, seeing nothing, followed after Fark.

"Oh shoot, I'm really in trouble now", muttered Glitch.

"Yes, indeed you are," replied Brett.

Chapter Twenty

The sudden change from the darkness of the cupboard to the light made Melody blink as she moved through the space where the wall had been, into the area beyond. It was Habitat 14 - no doubt about it. Just behind her, as she looked back to see where she had just come from, there was a sign embedded in the wall, "Unit 17, Habitat 14" and she realised, with horror, that she was looking at the wall through which she had passed. No turning back now - it was once again solid, but she was on the other side of it. She ran back and put her hands on the smooth white surface of the wall. There was no visible sign of a way to get back into The Outpost again. As she removed her hand, she saw that wall was actually covered in a light film of dirt that came off onto her hand, leaving a handprint where she had touched it.

She brushed it off and then decided to explore. *Jeeps, I'm not built for this sort of thing,* she thought as butterflies in her stomach showed her that her brain was probably shouting out a warning. She decided that she would ignore it and find what had happened to Xalata - she had to be in this area. The evidence of the buckle and just the fact that this was all so strange made her certain that she would find her.

But how am I suddenly in an area that's on Farside?

The question refused to go away. She could not possibly have travelled right around the Moon from The Outpost to here without TransTrak or a vehicle that would travel on or above the Moon's surface. She had appeared here instantly - impossible! She decided to shelve that little problem for thinking about later. Right now, she was on a mission.

She moved forward - the whole area of the Habitat seemed to be more dimly lit - maybe that was because of the layer of dust on everything. Parts of the atrium in which she stood looked as if a powerful force had blasted them. There were burn marks on the walls and some area had holes knocked through them, revealing spaces beyond. Most of all, there was no sign of people. It seemed unlikely that there would be because this part of the Habitat looked fairly unstable, although the pressure was holding up and there was no sign that this part had been breached. However, further along and into one of the corridors that went off the atrium, she found an airlock door that was firmly shut and locked with hazard warnings flashing upon it. Looking through the small window into the space beyond, she could see that it had been completely trashed and was open to the vacuum of space.

For one moment, she thought she saw a movement and there was a vibration as if something heavy had walked by on the other side of the door, but she could see nothing and the bumping disappeared and all was still once more.

As she moved back up the corridor and into the atrium once more, she noticed signs of wheel marks in the dust and footprints - one set large and two sets smaller. The footprints appear to show activity around the pairs of wheel marks but she couldn't really decipher what had happened there. Had people been arriving or leaving? The footprints themselves gave little indication of to whom the feet might belong, although the larger ones were evidently a bigger person. Who were they? Was this where Xalata was taken? If so, Melody could follow the tracks.

Suddenly, in the distance, she heard the low whine of a vehicle approaching and two voices talking. Without hesitating, Melody found a hiding place behind a low seat that was near one of the outer walls. The vehicle swept into the space - it was a standard, open low truck, powered by electricity, with a flatbed at the back for carrying loads and then four seats at the front, one of them for the driver, if a driver was needed. This type of truck was used everywhere in the habitats and they were charged wherever they were left, in small bays at various points around the areas. Melody ducked down behind the seat so there was no chance of being seen and before she could get a look at who was riding on the truck.

The two passengers were not talking as they came into the atrium, but, as they stepped off, they spoke again. Melody could only hear small fragments of what they were saying and she didn't recognize either voice. One was a man, and she thought she might know him but couldn't quite think why. The other could have been a man with a high voice or a woman with a low one.

"... make sure that she ..."

"... can't be certain ... why did he ..."

"... do as you're told ... will be serious for you ..."

The voices were getting heated and it was obvious that an argument was brewing. However, before Melody could hear any more, the two people moved off in different directions and one voice called out, "Back here in an hour and we'll get back to the secure base. Just watch your back!"

So, if they're going back somewhere in an hour, I'm going with them, thought Melody and she slowly lifted her head above the seat to see if anyone was still around. The two people had gone and the vehicle was left standing there. *I could steal it and follow the tunnel back the way they came in,* she thought, *but how would I know if they turned off?*

She decided that it was safer and more certain to hitch a secret ride on the truck so she darted quickly and quietly over to it to check out her options. Obviously she couldn't sit in the seats, so that left the flatbed of the back of the truck, which was covered in a plastic sheet. There were various bulges under the sheet where things that were being transported were taking up space. Between two bulges she could see that there was a good space and, when she pulled back the cover, she realised that it was even better. The two bulges turned out to be large cases containing tools, but there was a shallow well between them, which she would fit into very nicely indeed.

With less than an hour to go, Melody thought that she should probably think about getting hidden, in case one of the people returned early. She checked her bag, made sure she had everything with her, took a gulp of water from a bottle and then slid under the cover and pulled it back into place. It snapped shut as magnetic clasps found each other along the rim of the flatbed.

Although it wasn't very comfortable, there was space to move around and she found that she could sit up and check her pad without touching the cover at all. Her only worry was that the returning people would want to get something from under the cover or had more load to put on the truck. However, she was as far towards the seats as possible and the obvious place to put on additional stuff was at the back of the truck. She tried to relax and stop fretting.

She had only been under the cover a short while when she heard once more the thudding sound that she had heard behind the airlock door, when she had thought she had seen a movement. This sounded closer - a thudding noise as if something very heavy was constantly being lifted and dropped. She could feel small tremors through the floor and up into the vehicle and then, she heard something that made her blood run cold: a snorting and a low rumble as if from a massive beast like a dinosaur. It sounded as if it was in the atrium with her. Another snort came and a snuffling, followed by the sound of something very large moving around in the space. She was too scared to look out yet she desperately wanted to know what was out there.

Then, as more sounds of movement came closer, she felt the vehicle bump as something - the moving thing - hit it gently as it went past. She bit her hand to prevent herself from crying out in terror. There was a strange smell that worked its way under the cover - a chemical smell of minerals, mixed in with a pungent, almost animal, scent. Whatever it was out there was huge, moving and not very careful.

*   *   *   *   *

A little while later the sound of movement had faded away and it was obvious that whatever had been out there had now moved on. The remaining time before the two people were due to return passed slowly under the cover. She was bored and scared in equal measures but then, in the distance, she heard the two voices returning. Worried that they would find her, she made herself as small as possible in the well area of the truck. There was the sound of someone putting something heavy on the ground and then the unclipping of magnetic catches. *Oh cripes - they'll find me!* There was a thud and whatever had been carried to the truck was now put on the back and the catches were once more clipped in place. Melody carefully and quietly breathed a sigh of relief.

 She felt the truck's suspension drop a little as the two people got on board and then they set off. The ride was quiet, as no one was speaking. The vehicle hissed along, making no noise at all except for a hum from the wheels and the occasional gentle rattle as it passed over an area of rougher surface. The truck turned left and right and any attempt Melody was making to check the route was lost as it became too complex. She settled back in her space and tried to relax. There was still no sound from the two people on board and yet she was very aware that only an arm's length away from her were two individuals who would not be pleased to know she had stowed away. What would they do if they found her? She didn't dare go there and tried to think nicer thoughts as the truck hissed along the tunnels.

She had just been on the point of dozing off with the motion of the truck and the repetitive hum of its motor, when she felt it slowing down. After a couple of turns, the truck stopped and the two people got off, unloaded their package and walked away - she could hear their footsteps. At this point Melody took the opportunity to look from under the cover and caught a glimpse of two figures - a man and a woman it looked like, the man was carrying the package. Hopping down from her hiding place and keeping them at a distance, she followed and caught more glimpses of them - definitely a man and a woman. Their voices wafted back down the corridor - clearer now because of the acoustics of the tube through which they were walking.

"You check she's still secure and I'll take this lot and put it into the cold store. She'll not be needing it yet." Melody wished she could identify where she had heard the man's voice before. It was familiar and yet totally unlike anyone she knew.

"I don't want to keep going back to the main habitat," said the woman's voice, quite deep, but clear. "It's too dangerous. If we get caught by that thing it's the end."

"Don't be so worried, my dear. It will all be fine. We have the detectors and it can't reach where we go and hide. We need the supplies from down there as this end has been trashed. Now get going and make sure she doesn't see your face."

They arrived at an airlock door, which was obviously coded because they used a touchpad to validate themselves, and went inside. Melody couldn't follow so she settled down to wait, hidden from sight again. She was getting very hungry by now so she hunted in her bag for something to eat. An energy bar - she'd been one of the team at the Academy that had designed this particular one, all made from hydroponically grown foods. *I wish I was back there now and not doing this,* she thought miserably as she munched on the bar.

It wasn't long before the man and woman emerged from the door and headed back to the vehicle. As they drove away, Melody spotted another man coming down a different corridor and heading for the door. She was sure that through that door must be where Xalata was. As the man went in, she dashed across to stop the door sealing again. A dangerous move but she appeared to have got away with it.

Carefully, she went inside and allowed the airlock door to close. She stood with her back to the door and looked around to make sure she'd not been spotted. Then she tiptoed across the lobby that she found herself in, towards the doors at the end. One of these must contain Xalata! Just as she was nearing the end, she heard some more voices and, knowing the layout of these units, dashed back to a door that opened on a cupboard. Here she was again! The airlock hissed open and two more voices were talking about "the girl in Q10" and the fact that they needed to check her food in two days' time. Yep - it has to be Xalata.

OK - just need to get in there now, she thought as the voices faded again and the airlock door hissed shut. She pushed open the cupboard door and, now that she knew which room it was, she headed straight to the door labelled, Q10. The door had the usual arrangement of access pass plate and a touchpad to alert whoever was in there. Could she get Xalata to open the door if she pressed the plate? She tried and nothing happened. No sound. No motion. Nothing.

She looked around carefully. What to do? Then, having no better idea, she touched the plate again and, instantly, wished she hadn't. An alarm blared out, filling the lobby with noise so that Melody had to put her hands over her ears. She stumbled away from the door and headed back towards the cupboard, just as the airlock swung open and there stood two large masked men. And, judging by the way they were standing, they were not just coming on a shopping trip.

Chapter Twenty-one

Inside Q10, Xalata jumped up as she heard the alarm. A purple light was flashing on the door console but she had no idea what it meant. Running to it, she found that none of the controls would work, just as before. The noise was quite deafening and she found it difficult to think as the blaring alarm pulsed and wailed in her ears.

She glanced at the screen which showed the outside and, as she did so, she caught a glimpse of Melody - was that really Melody? - running away. *How could she be here?* she thought. *I'm somewhere on the other side of the Moon.*

She shouted out to try and catch Melody's attention, but of course she could not be heard through the thick airlock door. Then, without warning, two dark shapes appeared in the viewer and she realised that it was someone coming into the home. The airlock door opened sharply and two masked people came in. Boy, were they angry!

"Stop interfering with the door mechanism - you cannot escape, you stupid girl," said one of the men. "Set this alarm off again and we'll put you somewhere you really would not want to be, with something you really would not want to meet. Do I make myself clear?"

This last question was shouted and Xalata cowered back against the lobby wall, frightened by the power and threat of the man towering over her. When all was said and done, she was a 14-year old girl and these were hefty adults who looked as if they knew the inside of a gym. Then, in a flash of inspiration, she realised that these accusations were a great cover for Melody, if Melody it was, outside.

"I'm, I'm really sorry. I was just bored and, y'know, fiddling with stuff. I didn't realise I'd set off the alarms. I promise not to do it again - really. Shine a light - I'm only some girl, y'know. Really, really sorry ..."

"Yeah, shut up and just stop fooling about. Get back in the room." And with that, the two pushed her into the living space, marched back to the entry, shut the door and she heard the airlock close once more.

"Shoot. That was a bit hairy," and she crept back out to the lobby to check the viewer and see if she could see Melody again.

*   *   *   *   *

Melody watched the guards enter and then begin to leave again. She could hear raised voices as they came out of the home, but couldn't make out what was being said. She then realised that the guards had opened the door using a simple code. Without a moment's hesitation, she pulled out her pad to record what they entered on the control. Zooming in, she could just about see what was happening and recorded their exit. As they started to walk away, she checked back on the video and could make out five of the six numbers: 4-3-9-0-2 but she could not see the last one as one of the guards had moved in front of the control. There was no way she would risk entering the wrong number. It would certainly set off the alarm again and then who knew what trouble she and Xalata would be in?

She checked the video again to try and see whether she could work out which number had been pressed by the position of the body and hand. Still no luck. She just could not risk it.

Then she realised - each of the guards had a number on his uniform and one of them had 4-3-9-0-2 to start. The last number on the guard's own uniform was 2. It had to be the answer! The lazy guard couldn't be bothered to make a new code so had used his own personnel number. Idiot!

She waited until she was certain that all was clear and then she darted across to the door, punched in the code and waited as the door slid back. She couldn't believe her luck.

"What? Melody? But it's you," cried Xalata as she heard the airlock open and her friend walked in quickly. "I ... I'm speechless. For Frank's sake, how did you get here? What? I mean, this is Habitat 14 ..."

"I know," responded Melody, "I can't believe it myself," and she hugged her friend tight as they stood in the lobby. "Let's go into the living space," she continued, "In case they come back. At least I can hide then. Do you think they are watching you?" A horrible thought had occurred to Melody that the home may be being kept under surveillance.

"I don't believe so," said Xalata, "Cos there's no way out unless I know the code to the door ... but, you do though! Why don't we go?"

"Whoa! Hold on, where are you going to go? I don't even really know where we are, other than that it is across the other side of the Moon on Farside. How the freak we got here, I have no idea. But I came here under a cover on a truck."

"Me too. So, I didn't see anything as they brought me here."

"So, we need to know where we are going before we head off. We can get out of here any time we want 'cos I have the code. What we need to do is come up with a plan and, first, we need to know why they took you and what they want."

"I guess so," Xalata looked worried. "I've only been here a few days and already I'm causing my Dad trouble ... oh, no - does Dad know what's happened? He doesn't know where I am."

"No, he doesn't but I'm guessing we can soon tell him," and Melody pulled out her pad. "I'll just connect with him on The Q and get the cavalry to come fetch us!" And so saying, she tapped into her communicator and tried to contact Brett. Nothing happened.

"What? There's no connection. I can't see or speak to anyone."

"Maybe it's just in here. Should we try outside?"

"Too risky - there are people about out there and we can't take the chance that they see us going out of the airlock. There must be another way to get a message out ... but how?

Chapter Twenty-two

Glitch was fuming. His parents had grounded him and had made him stay in his room, telling him he was not to go to the Academy or leave the home. He had nothing to do and was bored out of his brain. He had tried to ping Xalata and Melody on his pad and had not had a response. He had also tried to track them by illegally tapping into the cameras that were everywhere around the area, but again, couldn't see anything. He didn't have permission to get into the historical records from the cameras although, he thought, it would not take a great deal to crack into them.

So, he sat. And he fumed. There was no one else around as his parents were at work. He'd been strictly forbidden from opening the door to any one or from stepping outside. It wasn't going to work, he decided. His friends were in danger - something weird was happening and he just couldn't sit on his hands while it took place. Besides, it was his fault in part, as he had lured Xalata to the dark doorway. He'd never realised that this was what had been planned and he felt a fool. His parents had been furious with him and, when he said about his sister on Earth being threatened, they had responded that she was fine - they had spoken to her only that morning!

He felt stupid, guilty and, above all, frustrated. He needed to DO something!

His pad sat beside him on the desk in his bedroom and he flipped idly through a number of areas of the habitat, hoping to pick up a clue, using the illegal access that he had worked out months ago to the network of cameras. Then he zoomed into the Outpost and followed the cameras backstage to where he had taken Xalata. The door could just be seen from the camera position he was in. As a cupboard it was innocuous, yet he knew that it was much more than a cupboard but he could not work out how it changed into the portal that he had seen as Xalata was snatched away.

As he looked, the door to the cupboard opened and someone stepped out. Glitch couldn't believe it - someone had actually been through from the other side and was now about to walk towards the camera. He held his breath and then let out a cry when he saw who it was. The walk was unmistakable - it was Fark! The chief of security looked both ways as he came out of the cupboard and then swiftly walked away down the corridor to the exit.

Glitch switched cameras and followed him all the way to the TransTrak, where Fark boarded a pod that was probably coming back to The Academy. *So, if Fark has just come out of the cupboard then he MUST know how the access through to the other side works*, thought Glitch. *The sneaky devil. All that when they arrested me was just show. He knew!* So what did that mean? Glitch racked his brains to try and make sense of the situation. One thing was certain, Fark was not on the side of the good guys.

Making a sudden decision, Glitch changed into dark clothes and then walked out of his room. He checked around the living area to see if there was anything else he needed, grabbed his pad from the bedroom. *I'm getting over to the Outpost so I can be there when he comes back,* thought Glitch. And, without hesitating he picked up the pad and walked out of the home, heading for the TransTrak.

*   *   *   *   *

When he arrived at the Outpost, the place seemed to be deserted. Even the usual security guys were not around so Glitch simply strolled through the door and headed backstage. *Here we go again,* he thought. The door to the cupboard was closed and Glitch stood outside, looking at it for a moment. Then he took hold of the handle and pulled it open, stepping inside.

The space inside was not particularly large - probably about four metres wide and three metres deep. Toward the right of the back wall there was a small alcove, formed by a section of protruding wall that probably housed pipework or something similar. Glitch realised that, in his dark outfit, he could hide in that space with little chance of being seen. He tried the space for size and found that he could fit in and be almost invisible inside the cupboard. Now all he had to do was to wait for Fark to make an appearance.

It was very dark inside the cupboard and Glitch found that his eyes soon became accustomed to the darkness. He looked around the space. There was really very little to see because the cupboard was empty. However, he suddenly noticed near the floor, there was a glass plate set into the wall. *Now what's that?* he thought and he bent down to check. As he did so, a strange sound filled the cupboard and a feeling of static electricity made his hair stand on end. There was a buzzing and a stretching almost as if his skin was being pulled from his face, then suddenly the room was filled with light and Glitch hurried back into his hiding place just as Fark entered the cupboard and stepped into Habitat 14.

Glitch sidestepped into the light and moved through into Habitat 14 behind him. He turned just as the lights dimmed behind him and then watched Fark stride away in the ruins of the habitat.

Okay. Here goes nothing. And with that he headed off to follow him.

Chapter Twenty-three

So, what to do? Melody and Xalata sat in the living space and looked at each other. They summed up their own situation:

"OK, we're locked up - but we know how to get out," said Xalata.

"Yep and we also know that somehow we are on Farside and that we came through some sort of portal that transported us from Nearside to here," added Melody.

"Sure and don't forget that we know that I was lured to the portal by Glitch - just wait till I see him, I'll break his neck ..."

"Not helpful, Xalata. Let's stick with the facts."

"OK then, Glitch sold me out to whoever grabbed me. They pulled me through the portal and then put me on a truck and brought me here, wherever 'here' is."

"We know that there are at least two of them 'cos there were two who brought both of us here and two people came when the door was locked. But, we don't know who they are or what they want of you - correct?"

"Yeah, but there may be more than two ..."

"Possible, but we have no way of knowing ... except, wait a minute. They have the numbers on their uniforms - they all wear security uniforms don't they. So we check the numbers to see whether we get more than one."

"Great plan - although personally I'd like to get out of here and avoid them totally. I don't know what they want me for, but it's not good."

"Sure, I understand that, but I think we need to know our enemy. It's no use just leaping in and hoping we can escape," said Melody. "Now, I think some food is in order. What say you?"

"Cripes, yeah, I'm starving ..." and with that they set about preparing some of the fast food packs that were stored in the fridge.

*   *   *   *   *

"That feels better," said Xalata, sitting back from the table after they had eaten their meal. It had been tofu with beansprouts and a soy sauce again, but she was already getting used to the hydroponically grown food that was the staple diet on the Moon. "So, brain-box, what have you thought as you munched?"

"Well," said Melody, "I think we need to know where these people are. They seem to walk around outside the home here so I don't think they are very far away. Also, there's something else I forgot to mention. They referred a couple of times to something nasty in the habitat and said they wouldn't want to encounter it ..."

"Yes, I heard something like that too. They threatened me that it wasn't safe outside or something similar."

"Well, while I was hidden under the cover in the truck, waiting to see where I would end up I heard all sorts of noises - a heavy movement and a sort of snorting. Don't know what it was 'cos I was too scared to look and also I didn't want them to spot me."

"Oh cripes - that doesn't sound good. What do you think it is? It couldn't be that creature that destroyed the place could it - didn't they find it and finish it off?"

"The Cryomorph. That was it," said Melody. "I don't know, but if it's not that, what is it for Frank's sake?"

"Don't really want to find out thanks," said Xalata, "All I know is we need to keep out of its way in that case. Anyway, what should we do?"

"Why are you asking me? I'm just the scaredy-cat around here!"

"Scaredy? Really? You've just blagged your way here through some sort of portal, hitched a ride with kidnappers, broken a code and come to my rescue. If you were a lad, I'd kiss you! Well, maybe ..."

"Well, I'm not and, when you put it like that, I suppose it was all a bit out of character. I was pooping myself all the time though!"

They both laughed at that and then suddenly realised that the situation was serious. They needed a plan, and fast.

Melody said, "We need to know about these two people so, I think when they come next, we should creep out after them and follow them. See where they go and what the lie of the land is."

"Well we know the lie of the land - the same as any other habitat, but just a bit more beaten up and abandoned."

"Yes, but we don't know where they are based, who they are, how many of them there are. I think understanding our enemy is the key to getting out of here. Anyway, even if we did find our way back to the portal, I wouldn't know how to open it - it had disappeared as soon as I turned around after passing through it."

They decided to wait it out and found a suitable hiding place for Melody for when the pair came back and then they settled down on the chairs, watching the big screen, which had a series of performances from Lunar Tunes showing.

"And if I don't get back soon, my chances of getting into the competition are tiny," said Melody. "Should have brought my guitar, so I could practise!"

*   *   *   *   *

About two hours later there was the sound of the airlock door being opened and Melody shot off to her hiding place. Xalata tried to look nonchalant as the two masked figures came into the living space. "Oh, hi there. Kidnapped anyone else at all? Could do with a bit of company here."

"You keep quiet, girl," said the taller of the two figures. "We need to make sure you haven't messed with anything else after the door incident. Just a quick check. Sit there and stay put." The two of them headed for the screen, checked its controls, examined the kitchen area - "You eat a lot for a girl."

"Yeah, well, I'm bored. I eat when I've nothing to do. Anyway, what's it to do with you? Get out of my face!"

"Listen, brat, we don't want to be here any more than you do so let's make with the nicey-nicey, huh? So's we can all just get along together. You'll be out of here as soon as we've got what we want. That is of course, assuming that we do get what we want."

"And if you don't ...?"

"Who knows, eh? We'll see soon enough. Now, we're going out that airlock and we don't want to see you anywhere near it. Come on F ... I mean, come on mate." With that, they headed for the door and closed it behind them.

Melody came cautiously out of her hiding place and whispered, "Have they gone." The hiss of the airlock confirmed they were already outside the home. "OK - let's do it!" and they both moved through the door to the airlock, checked the viewer and saw the pair moving out of sight.

"Quick!" said Xalata, "Put in the code." Melody checked her pad and entered the code in the door pad. The airlock hissed open and suddenly they were outside. "Lock it behind us too." Melody tapped in the code once again and then they both darted off in the direction in which the two people had vanished. Turning the corner, they saw them only a short distance away and then they turned suddenly down a corridor that obviously led to more homes.

Xalata and Melody ran up to the corner and looked around a moment before the pair entered the airlock on the end home. The last one through the door turned and looked back, not seeing the girls. "Oh, no! Got them," said Xalata and she looked back at Melody, "that was Fark!" As she looked at her friend with astonishment, she was just in time to see the shadow of a very large shape move across the wall behind them.

Chapter Twenty-four

Glitch had to be certain that Fark would not spot him so he stayed well back from him. It wasn't long before he completely lost him however as Fark seemed to disappear into thin air. *Great detective, I am,* he thought as he wandered around the dereliction. *Now what?* The habitat was in a mess with wreckage and rubble strewn around in places where the devastation had taken place.

He could see through into damaged areas that were exposed to the vacuum of space and suddenly realised that he was in some danger, so close to broken habitat. *Cripes, if any of these airlocks goes, I'm done for,* he thought and he headed away into the warren of tunnels, many of which were now poorly lit because of the ravages of the Cryomorph. It was creepy with dusty corridors illuminated by flickering lights, shadowy corners and doorways and, everywhere he went, strange footprints in the dust, marching ahead of him.

Mr Freeze, yeah. About as cool as a solar flare. What the freak are those marks? And, as he wondered, he heard from the depths of the tunnel network, a strange sound as if a great beast was stretching and waking. The noise terrified him, even though it sounded far away, but it also fascinated him too. Was it the Cryomorph that he had seen on the news updates? He'd do anything to get that on his pad to show his friends - amazingly cool! But, amazingly dangerous too and he wasn't sure he had the stomach for it.

His thoughts were interrupted as the sounds became suddenly louder as if the beast had turned a corner and come into much clearer hearing distance. *I need to hide!* And he dived behind an overturned unit that stood at an intersection between two corridors. Not a moment too soon for the ground literally shook as the great beast lumbered into sight, with Glitch peering through a crack in the broken furniture. It was huge, filling the tunnel with its bulk and swaying clumsily from side to side.

It didn't look quite the same as when he had seen it on the news update - it wasn't rampaging, but wandering as if it was a device that had lost its programming. It hauled itself down the tunnel opposite Glitch on its stumpy feet and then stopped, as if trying to sense his presence. It groaned - a deep rumble that reverberated in the confined space - and then backed up a little way, before turning down the tunnel to its right and thumping its way down the corridor, its sides brushing along the walls.

What's it doing? thought Glitch. *It doesn't seem to know where it's going. It's destroyed the environment but now has nothing to do - is it programmed?* Glitch intended to find out and he set off to follow it. Being brave, or perhaps foolish, he was able to approach it quite closely, working on the basis that it was unlikely to have eyes in its backside. He ran down the corridor quietly, being sure to stay out of its sightline as it swung its head back and forth. Then, all at once, he saw something that stopped him in his tracks. The Cryomorph really was controlled by something! A radio antenna and a control panel were embedded into the creature's back. *But where is it being controlled from and why is no one controlling it at the moment?*

He couldn't answer that one, but it was certain that it wasn't safe to be in the creature's sight and so he broke away at the next intersection as the Cryomorph lumbered off into the distance on its non-existent mission.

Just as it disappeared from sight, Glitch noticed wheel tracks on the floor, left in the dust from the wreckage and following a similar route to the one taken by the Cryomorph. *So there are vehicles here,* he thought to himself, *and I guess Fark picked one up as soon as he came through from Nearside. This will be the quickest way to track him down and see what he's doing.* Glitch quickly realised that if he followed the tracks back, they'd take him to a place from where the vehicles had started, so he followed them along the tunnels, retracing his steps a good part of the way, before forking off to the right into an area he had not seen previously.

At the end of a long corridor, lined with what had been offices, there was a small gallery housing a set of docking bays and, sure enough, there were two trucks charging in their bays and a couple of empty ones where trucks had been removed. The tracks that he had followed came straight into the first of the empty spaces. *OK, always wanted to whizz around the place in one of these and now's my chance!* And he hopped on board, studied the controls - one pedal for start and the other for stop - and pulled the vehicle tentatively out of its parking slot. It took only moments to get used to the controls and in moments he was retracing his steps, back to the badly damaged area where he had last seen the Cryomorph, then he followed the tracks, which inevitably must have been those of Fark's truck.

*   *   *   *   *

It was only ten or fifteen minutes later that Glitch came upon Fark's abandoned truck, parked in another charging bay, so he decided to park his nearby, but out of sight, giving him the option for a hasty retreat if he needed to do so. Jumping down, he surveyed his choices. The tyre tracks had of course stopped, but Fark's footprints were still visible. In any case, he was limited to going forward or going back so the decision was easy.

He set off for another five minutes and headed further into the tunnels, walking quickly because he needed to find some sort of habitation and, ultimately, what had happened to Xalata. Rounding another bend he found a section of larger structures that were intact. It looked like one of the main atriums of the habitat but, as he had not arrived in the place in the normal way, he had no real idea where he was, even though all the habitats were constructed in a similar pattern.

As he approached the buildings, he could see that there must be some sort of invisible barrier installed as he could see from the marks in the dust that the Cryomorph had not passed through an invisible line that ran across the floor, next to the buildings, even though there was an empty space to pass through. There were prints around the whole area, as though the beast had paced back and forth, trying to find a way in.

It must be a defence mechanism - he checked around the area where the marks stopped and tried to work out how the barrier worked. There was just a small sliver of plastic attached above the entry to the area - no bigger than a pen, but evidently full of clever electronics that kept the area secure - just the sort of thing that Glitch loved! Taking a small probe from his pack, he tested the device. It clearly was emitting some type of signal that would deter the Cryomorph from venturing any further.

With a quick flick of the probe, Glitch analysed the way the barrier operated and stored it for later study.

So what is in the rooms beyond that they need this type of protection? he mused. *Only one way to find out, I guess.* And with that, he pushed through the entry that, strangely, was not secured, followed the corridor a little further and found himself staring at a room full of equipment: screens, control surfaces, communications equipment for deep space - a command and control centre. But for what?

Locked on target

The loop around Venus had been completed and the asteroid was now on a closed trajectory to Earth. Only a reprogramming of its fusion thrusters could avoid an impact and the target was set: Beijing - one of the largest centres of uninfected population of Earth and the most important economically on the planet. More importantly, Beijing was the centre of the operations to terraform Mars and housed the agency that had built the LunarBase.

The hands that controlled the asteroid knew all this and their intent would soon become clear to the fools on Earth who dared to tamper with the ways of Asttar. The pre-ordained ways. The right ways.

The asteroid flew silently through the empty space that separated the planets; space that once was filled with many of its kind, before they all gathered together in clumps that formed the planets, many millennia before. Now, this lonely remnant from the birth of the solar system was going to be the agent of destruction of the one planet in the whole system that had borne life, that had spawned a technological civilisation that now was threatening to infect other planets with its progeny - human kind!

Chapter Twenty-five

"Holy shine-a-light, what the freak is that?" Xalata whisper-shouted back to Melody who was just turning as the shadow passed across the wall behind.

"Cripes! I dunno, but I don't want to be around to find out. Quick, let's find a place to hide ... here! Move it, for Frank's sake, it's coming!" The ground began to vibrate with the heavy steps of the creature that haunted the corridors of Habitat 14. As they dived for cover, the two spotted that the ground in front of their prison home was covered with strange marks in the dust - not just human boot prints including their own, but also the prints of a large beast, stopping in a quite clearly marked area, right in front of the home.

They crouched down behind a low wall that divided an ornamental display area from the rest of the corridor, near the junction with the main atrium. The Cryomorph, for such it was, pressed its huge bulk into the space next to the suite of homes. Immediately, the two friends had a chance to see the beast at close quarters and what a sight it was.

Its small head was totally out of proportion to the massive body, which lumbered along on four stout legs that resembled those of an elephant, but without the grace or flexibility of that noble creature. The head was covered in bumps and lumps that gave it a diseased look and its nose and mouth reminded them of those of a pig from their home planet. Above the ears and pointing forward, were two gnarled horns that seemed to serve little purpose - except Melody and Xalata had seen the news update where the security camera had captured the creature blasting its way through walls in the habitat, seemingly impervious to the consequences of the destruction it wrought. Those horns were twin antennae that delivered a massive capability to destroy things with electricity.

The rest of the beast's body was covered in a folded pale grey hide that looked tough and impervious, with carapaces and armour to protect the sensitive connections between neck and body and between the legs and the body. The whole thing moved stiffly, but its bulk belied its speed as it twisted sharply to face some imagined enemy and then turned back to its solitary wanderings.

"I've never seen anything like it!" whispered Xalata.

"Shhhh! For Frank's sake, we don't know how good its hearing is," and, as if it had heard their exchange, the Cryomorph swivelled and stared in their direction, peering with its tiny eyes. The two girls pressed themselves lower behind their hiding place and prayed that it would go away. Suddenly, they felt a pressure from the frame of the divider behind which they were crouching - the beast was pushing it as if trying to remove it and see what was behind it. Xalata stifled a scream and Melody wrapped her arms around her friend as if to protect her. The unit moved, sliding on the shiny floor and the girls shuffled with it, maintaining their position out of sight, until they were backed up against the wall.

Without warning, Melody jumped up, shouted out loud and then rushed down the corridor opposite, back into the atrium. The Cryomorph saw her and swivelled once again to follow with its eyes. Sharply turning, it dashed after her, its feet pounding the ground in an efficient yet graceless locomotion that sent it wheeling after the running girl.

Xalata sat, astonished at her friend's foolishness. "Melody!" she yelled at the top of her voice and stood up to give chase. Then she realised that, if she did so, she was putting herself in danger of being attacked by the Cryomorph as well: not something she fancied.

She could hear the rumble of its progress around the habitat as it pursued Melody, but she realised that Melody had been clever. She could turn, manoeuvre, and get through spaces that the Cryomorph could not navigate. She hoped against hope that her friend would be able to outwit the clumsy, yet dangerous creature.

Her wishes were fulfilled when, with a triumphant yell, Melody burst into the space where Xalata was standing, open-mouthed. "Easy-McPeasy! That thing couldn't catch a cold. I just outran it."

"Are you completely, utterly, stark, starry-eyed, staggeringly stupid? You could have been killed," gibbered Xalata.

"Nah, no chance. I lost it and we can get on with our investigation." As she said those words, the corridor ahead became blocked by the bulk of the returning Cryomorph. And it didn't look pleased to see them.

Chapter Twenty-six

Fark marched at top speed round a corner to a cart, jumped aboard and then set off down the tunnels to head to the Control Centre. The mission was reaching a critical point and it was important that everyone involved stayed focused so that the target was achieved. He detested the Moon and everything that was happening on it - in fact, his aim was to destroy everything that mankind was trying to do: colonising the Moon and then leaping off to the planets with the aim of making places which were habitable for humans.

"Fools!" he muttered to himself as the cart sped through the white corridors, navigating by itself. "Wasn't the plague that was unleashed upon us enough to make people think that we were on the wrong path? No! So, what do we do? Go off to infect our own Moon and then on to the rest of our sacred Solar System."

There was a wild look in his eye and he ranted more and more loudly until the corridors echoed with his voice as the cart dashed through them. "The will of Asttar be done!" he cried and waved his fist in the air. As he did so, the cart turned sharply to the left and a large atrium came into view. It slowed down and came to a stop next to an airlock door that was labelled, RESTRICTED AREA - AUTHORISED PERSONNEL ONLY.

Fark stepped from the cart, approached the airlock and faced a small camera set into a panel on the side. His eye was scanned and after a moment a clunk indicated that the door was now unlocked. He pulled on the locking lever and swung open the door then stepped inside, closing it gently behind him. Confident that no one else would intrude, he didn't bother to lock it as he would not be in the Control Centre for long.

The room was quite compact, with a number of large interactive status screens that showed the progress of the mission. The trajectory of the asteroid was clearly marked and the changes in its route could be seen in the trail that led up to the present position. Now, the forward trajectory curved around to target the Earth and, as he watched, Fark could see that settings were constantly changing as the navigation code monitored and updated the route on a second by second basis.

He moved over to one of the panels and studied the detail of the impact time, the likely Impact speed and the energy output that would result from the asteroid hitting the Earth. He nodded and smiled to himself as he saw that everything was going to plan.

Meanwhile, on another screen, he could see frantic activity down on Earth where the Beijing Control Centre was desperately trying to regain control of the asteroid. It was clear that they could see what was happening and, of course, they could see the same read-out as he could. The same clever algorithms that had locked them out of the navigation had given him absolute control of the asteroid and its fusion engines. He chuckled as he saw their desperate plight - yes, they knew what was happening - the asteroid would be hitting Beijing in a matter of 15 hours.

And there was nothing that they could do about it!

Satisfied, he made a few minor tweaks, locked down the system once more and then headed for the door. *I need to get back to speak with that idiot, Brett,* he thought, *so I had better get back before I am missed.*

Chapter Twenty-seven

Xalata and Melody froze in horror as the Cryomorph stood in the entrance to the corridor. It fixed them with its tiny eyes and then leaned back a little as it prepared to charge them. Xalata suddenly realised that if they stayed put they'd be mincemeat and she grabbed Melody's arm and pulled her bodily towards the entrance to the home.

"Get behind here - it can't come past!" she yelled as she dragged her open-mouthed friend behind the line marked by the device overhead.

"I'm so sorry," gasped Melody, "I thought I had outrun it and that it would simply wander off again." I could have killed us!"

"Don't be nuts, you just underestimated it." As Xalata spoke, the Cryomorph crouched, ready to charge towards them - the girls, wide-eyed, watched it with naked fear in their eyes. It left the tunnel like a bullet, its feet pounding the dusty floor, driving it at them with terrifying speed and then, at the last moment, it broke away to the left as it was unable to pass the barrier. "See, no problem. I love tech!" said Xalata and she turned and headed back towards the home, looking much more chilled than she felt. "Let's have a drink before we go anywhere. This excitement has left me parched."

Melody unfroze from her braced position and gave a watery smile. "I don't ever want to see anything like that. Not ever again."

*   *   *   *   *

Ten minutes later, they emerged from the home having snacked on juice and an energy bar and discussed the sighting of Fark. "Right, let's go hunting!" said Xalata and she led the way back, watching out for signs of the Cryomorph, to where they had spied on the two people disappearing into another home. There was no sign of activity - the area was empty, as indeed the whole of the habitat seemed to be, but they knew that their captors were potentially behind that door so they planned to wait and see them emerge. Finding a suitable hiding place in a small alcove next to a little-used corridor, "Look, no footprints!", they didn't have long to wait.

Out from the home came an unmasked figure that Xalata instantly recognised. She gasped and clutched her mouth to prevent any noise coming out. "It's Castrana Machin," hissed Xalata.

"And," whispered Melody, "she's the one who was holding the lecture in the Outpost, isn't she?"

"Let's hope she's not going back to check on me - there'll be trouble if she does."

"No - she's turning the other way - quick, let's keep up," and the two friends left their hiding places and crept to the corner where they had seen the woman turn. She was about 100 metres ahead at this point so the girls felt reasonably safe following at a distance, ducking into doorway alcoves or peeking around corridor entries in order to stay out of sight.

After following for a few hundred metres they saw Castrana open an airlock and enter an area that was obviously off limits to everyone else. The sign on the door made that quite clear. As the airlock hissed shut behind her, the two girls dashed up to it and tried to peer inside through the glass porthole fixed in the top of the door. They could see very little and so sat down near the entry to try to work out what was happening.

"OK, here's what I don't get," said Xalata. "The Cryomorph does a great job of trashing what is actually an already abandoned habitat. It's been made or grown or whatever, by someone to do that job. Make any sense so far?"

Melody shook her head. "Nope, don't get it yet."

"All right. That's clear then. So, I get kidnapped and locked up - presumably by Fark and Castrana Machin, but not on Nearside. They bring me all the way across here through a magic portal that works, I don't know how. Yep?"

Melody nodded.

"We don't know why I've been kidnapped - is it for ransom? We don't have any money I know of. Or is it for something else?"

Melody just looked at her feet. "Maybe Glitch knows something as he was the one who led you to be captured?"

"Don't think so. He looked absolutely terrified when I was grabbed. I think he was bullied into it somehow. Anyways, then we just see Machin - what's that about? And they are doing something behind this door that we can't get through - we could try that same passcode as before, but it's a bit risky. Oh, meanwhile, our friend Mr Fark's supposed to be in charge of keeping this all safe, isn't he? And, all in all, it's a bit of a puzzle. "

Melody laughed, "Yeah, master of understatement there! The problem is, what can we do about it? We don't know how to get back to Nearside - it's so far away - and the portal just disappeared. There must be a way to get it back because, if you think about it, if Fark is here, he must be going through it too!"

"Yep, and that means that he can skip back and forth across the Moon without anyone really knowing that he's missing. Cunning! Know what I think? We should go back to the home where I'm being held and just chill out a bit until we get more data to help figure this out. If they find I'm missing, then the cat's out of the bag and we can't do anything except be hunted down. Frank knows what the Cryomorph can do if they take it off its lead. We're safer back there."

"OK," said Melody, reluctantly, "But we're just going to be sitting and waiting for something to happen?"

"Yep - you got a better idea?"

"Nope."

Chapter Twenty-eight

Brett was at work when the message came through from the kidnappers:

Your brat is safe, for the moment. She's where you'll never find her - don't bother trying. Put your effort into fulfilling our requirements: 1. You know what we want and if you don't you're stupid - you will provide us with a consignment of 60kg to be delivered to a specific location on further instructions. 2. You will surrender yourself to us willingly and do as we say. 3. You will remain silent and not inform any authority of these demands. Failure to follow these requirements will result in a very unpleasant end for your kid. Please don't think that these are idle threats. Others have challenged us before and suffered the consequences.

We shall be in touch. Be prepared to leave at short notice.

Brett sat back at his desk and reread the message. It had come through to his pad from an untraceable address and had no signature, no identification of any sort. He'd been expecting it of course, but that didn't make the blow any easier when it landed. He needed to show it to Fark and get his view on it. Whatever happened, he wasn't going to say no, because he could not put Xalata in danger, no matter what the downside was.

He buzzed Fark but got no response. *Strange*, he thought, *I'm sure Fark is around here somewhere*. And he set off to try to find him inside the Institute. No one had seen him. In fact, the last anyone remembered was that Fark had disappeared in the direction of the TransTrak. *So where was he going? His duties are here ...* Brett was puzzled but his mind was too full of everything else to get in too much of a stew. He needed to think how they could respond, how they could get Xally back and how the criminals who were doing this could be brought to justice.

"Mr Orbit?" A voice brought Brett out of his thoughts. It was Wiglet.

"Ah, Mr Wiggins. Just the person ..."

"Oh? I was rather concerned because two of my students appear to have gone missing."

"Two?" said Brett with surprise. "I thought it was only one."

Wiglet looked at him with a strange expression, "How do you mean, only one? Do you know what has happened to them?"

"Er, no. No, sorry. I was thinking of something else. Xalata is, um, unwell and is at the home recovering. Who else is missing?"

"I think you might have let me know, Mr Orbit. The other missing person is Melody Fret - she was last seen dashing out of the Academy and heading for the TransTrak."

Strange. Was she going the same place that Xalata went and where Glitch led us? thought Brett. "I'm sure I don't know. Girls sometimes take it into their heads to do strange things. I'm guessing she will be around very soon." *I must check with her mother whether she has any news of her.* And so saying, Brett said goodbye to Wiglet and headed off to find Dawn Fret, Melody's mother.

Dawn had been one of the pioneers of lunar habitat living. She and her husband had come to the colony in the early days and had brought their young child, Melody, with them. She had known little else other than life on the Moon although she had been to Earth a few times on trips to see family and friends. But all of them actually preferred the lunar way of life and had become accustomed to its restrictions and problems. Sadly, Dawn's husband had died ten years previously, not long after they had moved to the habitat. She had carried on their work alone, knowing that the alternative was to go back to a fairly dull life on the still-dangerous Earth.

Brett found Dawn in one of the labs in the engineering section of the Institute. She was a pretty lady of about 38, with short-cropped blonde hair and an engaging smile that lit up her otherwise serious face. Dressed in a lab coat that looked a couple of sizes too big for her, she was quite small in height, but was evidently Melody's mother, as she had similar facial features.

She worked on nano-technology, getting tiny machines to build and replicate the structures and systems that were needed for lunar living. Nanobots could be programmed to do practically anything, using the available materials on the Moon's surface and so they had been developed to create the tunnels of the TransTrak, build the habitats and create technology that helped people live a reasonably normal life, far from the home planet.

"Dawn, sorry to interrupt your work ..."

"No, no problem Brett - great to see you. We haven't had a chat for months."

"No - I know. Life has been busy. Er, I just wondered, is Melody OK?"

"Yes, as far as I know. Why do you ask?

"She's not at the Academy at the moment and Wiglet was asking where she was. Xalata is not there either so I think he was concerned. Um, Xally is at home - bit of a bug, I think."

"Not at the Academy? Where's she gone? I'll check her pad ..."

"I've already tried. She's not responding."

"Bizarre. I had better go back home and check."

"Well, I'm just going back to ours so I could drop in if you like - save you the trip. I'll ping you if I find anything."

"Yes, OK, I suppose that's a good idea. I'll give you a guest passtag that will let you in. Call me when you've had a look, would you? I can't imagine what that girl could be doing. She's normally so good," and she handed Brett a small disk that would let him in.

"Sure thing." Brett hurried away, eager to take a look. He didn't know why, but he thought he might find a clue as to what was happening. The place where Glitch had said that Xalata had been captured just didn't add up. Unless.... surely not? He'd heard that there was portal technology on the Moon, but no one had ever indicated where it might be or who might have it. It certainly wasn't official - and never would be, in fact it was illegal except for special tasks that were limited to top-secret projects. Portals were far too dangerous to be used for anything that regularly involved humans. The technology often failed and when it did, the consequences were disastrous for anybody caught in the flux.

But what Glitch had described sounded awfully like it. His worries instantly doubled.

Chapter Twenty-nine

Fark emerged from the portal and dashed back to the TransTrak to get back to the Institute before he was missed. Brett would be jumping up and down now, having received the ransom note so Fark needed to be there to play the concerned Security Chief - security! Hah! It was a joke. These scientists wouldn't know security if it bit them on their backsides, but of course, that was the strength of the Asttarian's plan. They could take advantage of the scientists' naiveté and so manage to fulfil their own plans without any major problems.

Kidnapping Xalata had seemed the only way though to get the supplies of lithium that the group needed for the secret and illicit development work that was taking place on Farside, far away from prying eyes. Security on Nearside was so tightly secured that even Fark couldn't get past the barriers, checks and balances - most of which he'd set up himself, whereas Brett could call it out of the store whenever he needed it to use as part of the air supply system chemicals. It wasn't held in the form of lithium that they wanted - it was mostly as salts, so it needed extracting. And if a job like that needed doing and you had scientists on hand, what better way than to blackmail or bludgeon one of them into doing it for you, on the quiet?

He stepped from the TransTrak and walked over to the Institute main entry only to walk into Brett. "My dear, Brett. How wonderful to catch you - has there been any progress with Xalata? Has she appeared yet? I can't believe that that boy, Shaw-Storey, could make up such a tale!"

"No sign yet, Adolf, I'm afraid."

"I know our teams have been working as hard as possible to trace her, but as yet there are no clear leads. In my view, we should interrogate the Shaw-Storey boy again and establish what he really knows. That nonsense about a door inside the cupboard - it sounds like a children's story! I'll put that in place and have him brought in for some close questioning ..."

"Before you do that, Adolf, I'd like to show you something back in my office. Do you mind?"

"Of course, dear boy, no problem at all. At your disposal." Fark was at his most oily and Brett was not convinced by his tone, or by the fact that he had suddenly gone off the grid for a couple of hours. However, he would question him later on that. The priority now was to find Xalata and to discover who could possibly have sent the note. And, more importantly, how was he going to respond to it?

*   *   *   *   *

They arrived in Brett's office and both men sat down, facing each other across the small conference table that took up part of the confined space.

"It's really strange. Disappearing like that. Was Xalata an unstable type at home on Earth?"

Brett looked at Fark sharply. "What do you mean by that?"

"Well, was she inclined to run off, be disobedient and so on? She seems to me to be a fairly wilful girl ..."

"How she seems to you is irrelevant, Adolf," Brett deliberately mispronounced his name. "What's important is what the security services are doing - because to my mind, it's not a lot."

"My dear boy ..."

"Enough of the 'dear boy' stuff, I've a daughter who's lost somewhere and now I have received a note from who knows whom, telling me that I have to jump through hoops to get her back! Now, what are your team doing about it?" Brett was getting angry and he was still not sure what his view was of Fark.

"Well, I must say that I find your attitude a little strong, my d ..., erm, Brett. We have worked together for some time and my care for you and for your daughter are self-evident. Now this note demanding that you jump through hoops, as you put it, and remain silent, that's quite another matter. We shall need to examine that forensically to determine where it came from and ..."

"I'm perfectly capable of doing that myself," snapped Brett. "And where have you been for the past couple of hours? I was trying to contact you."

"Ah, I was cloistered with some of my surveillance team, trying to work back on the security footage that was taken during the time the girl disappeared."

"Xalata."

"Yes, exactly. Xalata."

"You seem to be depersonalising this matter, Fark, and for the life of me I can't think why."

"Depersonalising, hardly. The dear girl is the very focus of my attention."

"And your surveillance team have found what exactly?"

"Erm, well, it's too early to say at this point. They need to run some tests on the recordings and check that what they are seeing is accurate ..."

"Why?"

"How do you mean, 'Why?'"

"Why do they need to check back on the recordings - they either show what happened or they don't, wouldn't you think?" Brett's voice was raised now and Fark sat uneasily in his chair. "In fact, I don't believe that you've been with your team today, despite what you say. Where you've been, I'm not sure, but I think you were up to no good and I'm going to dig until I find out. Oh, and by the way, I never mentioned that the note had told me to keep quiet - you seemed to manage to intuit that all on your own. How clever!"

Fark leapt from his seat and dashed to the main door, but he was not as quick as Brett who grabbed him by the scruff of the neck and dragged him back to the chair on which he had been sitting.

"Sit there, Fark. I want some answers and I shall get them. Move and you'll regret it." *My goodness*, thought Brett, *I'm sounding like something off a cheap movie.*

He stepped towards the kitchen area, keeping his eyes on Fark and dug around in one of the lower drawers to find a roll of tape. "Gaffer tape, Fark. The greatest invention ever made by man. Repair anything. Hold anything. Secure anything - including you." At that moment, Fark's communicator buzzed and both men looked at it as he pulled it from his pocket. "Well it's not me, Fark, so I guess it's one of your evil henchmen! Answer it and make sure I can hear both sides of the conversation."

Chapter Thirty

The girls were, frankly, bored out of their skulls. They had finished chatting and knew that sitting in the home, waiting for someone to show up was getting them nowhere. Yet, as Xalata had said, if she was discovered to be missing by the bad guys, then there would be a pack hunt for her, probably led by the Cryomorph.

"I've got it!" she cried suddenly.

"What? What's the matter," Melody was startled by the sudden shout and turned to face Xalata.

"If we make it look as if I *am* still here, even when I'm not, then we can buy ourselves some time and go and get on with finding out what the freak is going on here."

"Yeah, ok. And how are you intending to do that?"

"Well, we make a dummy in one of the beds that looks like me. There are some clothes here so I'll change into them, put the dummy in my clothes and then wrap it in the bedclothes to look as if I'm still here!"

"Genius ... not," scoffed Melody. "You think that'll work? They'll see through it in a moment."

"No they won't. I'll leave a message saying something along the lines of 'Got bored and went to bed. Not feeling well - I think your food is crap.'"

"Hmm. OK, maybe it's worth a try. But just remember that I'm fresh out of ideas for keeping the Cryomorph at bay."

"Oh, I'm not. I know just how we'll do it. C'mon. Let's make that dummy." And Xalata ran off into the bedroom to change.

*   *   *   *   *

Fifteen minutes later, with Xalata's old clothes stuffed with bedding, towels and other assorted cloth from around the home, plus a head fashioned from a cleaning mop, the bed was occupied by a Xalata clone. The bedclothes were pulled up cleverly, exposing parts of the clothing and the top of the "head" and, with the lights dim, it looked reasonably convincing, at least on a quick look.

"Great job!" said Xalata as she closed the bedroom door and scribbled a note on the cooler screen. "That should do it. Now, let's make tracks." And with that, she led Melody to the airlock door, opened it with the code and crept out, looking to left and right in case of the return of Fark and Machin or, worse still, the Cryomorph.

They headed straight back to where they had last seen Castrana Machin, taking care not to be spotted. Once they arrived, eyes open all the time in case the pair who had gone in came out of the airlock door, they hid once more behind part of the building fabric that added a small amount of decoration to the entry to the building.

"So what do we do now? How are we going to get in there to see what's happening?" whispered Melody. "I just don't see how we can get past them without them noticing."

"I think we can manage it," said Xalata. "First off, we try the code that they used for the home where I was locked up. People are lazy about stuff like that. And, let's just look back at the number on the other suit in my video - I suppose it was Castrana Machin as she was the smaller one. They might use that. That gives us two chances. My guess is we'd get three goes before the alarm goes off. And, if it does, we'll beat it."

"OK," said Melody, doubtfully. "I'd prefer not to risk the code thing. They might use something completely different or even a biometric pass on here, like a thumbprint or an retina scan."

"Yeah, well, you know what the answer is then, if that's the case?"

"No. What do you mean?"

"We'll need to get the thumb! Or, better still, the eyeball!" Melody shuddered in disgust while Xalata laughed at her own joke. "Right, let me recall that video," and Xalata opened her pad and scanned for the film that featured the two masked characters. "Yep, look, here. I can see the whole number. We ignored it because we didn't notice it in our excitement. This'll zoom and show us for sure. There you go - 442678." She noted it down and then closed her pad. "Now we just need the opportunity, assuming they're still in there."

Nothing much happened for several minutes as the two friends discussed their options and waited for the two crooks to appear. They were just beginning to despair, when there was a hiss and the airlock door opened. Out walked Machin, along with another person they didn't recognise - a man with dark hair and skin, wearing a white lab coat.

"We'll leave it for the day," said Castrana Machin to the man. "The girl is stowed away safe and sound and she can't make any more trouble. Fark is back at the ranch so he'll be dealing with the Orbit guy and the blackmail note. Nothing more to do at the moment until we get a result from Orbit. I'll see you back here at oh-eight-hundred."

"OK," said the lab-coated man. "See you then."

The two girls waited until the pair had left the area and then snook out of their hiding place and approached the airlock.

"Here goes nothing," said Xalata and flipped open a security plate on the door and punched the new code from the video straight into the keypad. Nothing happened.

She was about to try it again, when Melody said, "Look, the door's not been closed - it's standing ajar." Sure enough, the airlock had not been resealed and there was apparently no need to enter a code to gain entrance.

"These guys are very sloppy. They're used to having no one around so they're not using their security procedures. All to our advantage!"

They quietly pulled the heavy door and it slid open silently, then they pulled it half-closed behind them, as they would undoubtedly need the security code to get out again if it was closed properly. The area was half-lit until they began to move forward and automatic lighting kicked in, showing the way to a series of doors. There was evidently no one in the area as the lights had already dimmed.

They pushed against the nearest door and were surprised to see a brightly lit control room. Entire walls screened the readouts from instrumentation and a large transparent screen faced across the room on a raised platform where someone evidently controlled operations. On one wall, stars shone from a skyscape that Xalata instantly recognised from her astro-navigation classes on Earth. "That's showing our solar system from the perspective of Jupiter," she muttered. "But why?" As they watched it was evident that the scene was changing in tiny steps and she suddenly realised that it was a viewpoint from some space vehicle that was travelling through the solar system. "So what is it? Where's it going?"

Melody meanwhile, had gone up to the large control screen and was studying the options that were presented on it. Navigation tools were there, along with systems that were making rapid calculations on a three-dimensional star map. She touched the screen and the virtual device under her finger sprang to life, pulling itself up to dominate the screen and showcase the detail of the data that it had been only summarising while it was in a semi-dormant state. She peered intently at it, "This is a navigation control for some sort of space vehicle that's on a course that I don't understand."

"Let's see," said Xalata and she sprang up on the platform to look. "What's this panel here?" and she touched another area of the screen, which jumped up to show a detailed view of the planet Earth. A trajectory line showed a path from space onto the Earth's surface and, as Xalata moved her fingers over the model and zoomed into the target area, she could see that the end of the line was Beijing, China, heart of the planetary development programme. "So, whatever is flying through space is going to land in Beijing. It's probably an exploration craft that's been on a long voyage outside the solar system, collecting data on planets circling nearby stars. Mind you, that would be a very old craft, if that's the case. Even with newer fusion drives and travelling at say half the speed of light, it would take many years to get there - and that's if it went to our nearest star!"

"Well, thanks for the astro lecture," grinned Melody. "I'm much wiser, I'm sure. So, we still don't know what it is, where it's coming from, but we *do* know where it's going."

"Sure thing, now, what's this panel?" Xalata tapped another area of the screen and a dark, rocky landscape met their eyes. Behind it, a tapestry of stars moved very slowly, but quite clearly. "What the ... what's this? It looks like a part of the Moon, but it's moving. I don't get it." Just for a moment, in one corner of the image she saw a bright flash of light that was there and then gone again. "And what was that? It looked like a flame, but I can't be sure. There's no volcanic activity on the Moon. I'm baffled."

"Oh my," gasped Melody. "I know what it is. Holy freak! It can't be - my mum told me about this. It's a part of the terraforming programme for Mars. It's a freakin' asteroid!"

"What do you mean, an asteroid? It's moving."

"Yes, it's got fusion engines built on to it and they are moving it to hit Mars."

"Why?"

"The asteroid contains lots of minerals that are good for the terraforming process - you know what that is, don't you."

"Yeah, of course - we go to Mars and we make its atmosphere like the Earth's by making it warmer with greenhouse gases like carbon dioxide and methane. Then we put in living organisms like bacteria that let us start growing stuff rather than just doing the hydroponics thing - I have been listening in classes you know!"

"Well the asteroid is part of the process: we capture the asteroid, drive it towards the planet with the fusion engines and then let it hit the surface. This throws up all sorts of minerals and chemicals like ammonia as well as releasing water and other stuff from beneath the surface of the planet. It's ever so risky, but this programme is working with the rest of the terraforming to make it all happen quicker."

"Yeah. OK, I get it. So why is its route targeting Beijing?"

"Exactly!"

Chapter Thirty-one

Fark held the communicator in his hand and touched the screen. A voice came through clearly and a face was visible - the same guy in the white lab coat as had been seen by Xalata and Melody on the other side of the Moon.

"Boss, all's clear. The mission's on target and the girl's locked away. She'll not be disturbing anyone." Fark looked towards Brett who had a face like thunder. "Answer him," Brett mouthed so that the other man couldn't hear him.

Fark looked back at the communicator. "Thank you, Sparkes. I'm sure everything is under control."

"You OK boss?"

"Why, yes. Just a little tired I think."

"You seemed a bit distracted. Sure everything's OK that end? Did you find that meathead, Orbit?"

Fark blinked and then responded, "Er, yes, I did and I shall be speaking with him shortly."

"OK, boss, that's fine. Keep him strung along. He'll never guess!" Sparkes laughed and then said, "I'm off for my dinner. I'll call if there's anything to say."

"Thank you, yes. That would be marvellous." The call finished and Fark looked at Brett.

"Meathead, eh? Is that what you think of me?" Fark didn't reply. "Right, let's get you secure," and, with that, Brett grabbed hold of the smaller man, dragged him to a chair and was about to start to wind the gaffer tape around him when Fark suddenly swung his elbow back, caught Brett a blow on the side of the head and then made a dash for the airlock door.

Momentarily stunned, Brett staggered and then recovered and with a great bound, leapt after Fark as he tried to open the door. "Guess my workouts in the gym are paying off, you little toad. I ought to floor you, but I'm not going to drag myself down to your level." He dragged him back to the chair and Fark seemed to collapse, all the fight gone from him. Brett steadily wrapped the broad tape around Fark's arms and the chair arms and then around his legs and the chair legs. "You're not going anywhere for a while," he muttered under his breath as he worked. "Now, let's see what's in your communicator."

A look of terror came over Fark, but he didn't say a word, just sat bound to the chair, looking at the floor.

"What's certain," continued Brett, "is that you are a bad guy and we know what happens to them in the movies don't we? The question is, what sort of bad guy are you?" He picked up the communicator, walked over to a desk at the other side of the living space and pulled out some electronics from a drawer. "This should help answer that question."

He connected the communicator to the tools and sat back to wait for the results. "I use these for decrypting signals from space so I don't think your poor attempts at encryption will baffle me for long," and he pulled out a number of documents onto his pad, which he then proceeded to study.

"So, there is something in that cupboard at the Outpost, after all. And it looks suspiciously to me like a portal - that would chime in with what the Shaw-Storey kid said when we interviewed him. You do know this technology is dangerous and illegal, don't you?" Fark continued to study the floor. "So I'm guessing that Xalata is on the other side of that doorway, wherever that might lead. Where does this particular wormhole come out, Fark?"

"You'll just have to find out for yourself, won't you? You don't know what you're messing with here, Orbit. If you don't let me go, you'll never see your nasty little daughter again."

Brett took a step towards him and Fark flinched, expecting a blow. "You're not worth the calories, Fark. If you think that I am not going after my daughter, you're completely nuts. And whatever operation is going on behind this, you can be sure I shall expose it. I'm making a guess - and it may be a wild one - but I reckon you might be part of these idiots, the Asttarians. And, if that's the case, I've a very good idea where that wormhole comes out."

Brett stepped away and headed for the door, "I have to check on Melody - she's not turned up at the Academy either and..." The realization of what he was saying was suddenly evident in his face. "Melody must have gone to look for Xalata. She's probably with her."

"Don't be ridiculous," said Fark. "That mouse? She's too frightened to do anything. She'll be at home with a headache."

"We shall see!" said Brett and stepped out of the airlock, securing it behind him. He ran up the corridor to Melody's home and touched the door alert. There was no answer so he used the guest passkey given to him by Dawn Fret, moved through the airlock door and walked into the living space. The place was empty. He poked his head around the bedroom doors - no sign of anyone. Opening his communicator, he called Dawn and let her know that Melody was not there.

"I can't think where she would be," said Dawn, the anxiety now clear in her voice. "I'm coming home."

"I don't think there's much point," said Brett. "However, I think I might know where she is. I told you a small untruth today, Dawn. Xalata's not at home either. Something strange is going down and it involves those two girls. I'm looking into it now, so can you just wait on my next call and we'll see whether my suspicions are right?"

"What do you suspect them of doing, Brett? They're such good girls..."

"It's not they who are the problem, but I'll need to confirm what I'm thinking. Give me a couple of hours. Don't contact anyone at the moment and certainly don't contact Fark!"

"Why ever not?"

"Tell you later..."

Chapter Thirty-two

The two girls stared at the screen and could see that the asteroid was winging its way towards the Earth with Beijing as its target. What could they do to stop it? Xalata scanned the screens, touching places where there seemed to be controls, but failing to understand how they worked.

Melody stood by, looking desperate. "There must be something we can do, surely?"

"I don't know. The controls don't make a lot of sense to me. Did you say that the asteroid's supposed to be hitting Mars?"

"Well, yes, that's what my Mum told me. She's saying it's part of the..."

"Yeah, terraforming project - you said already. The question is, why's it now heading for Earth and who's made it take this new course? And, how do we put it back on target?"

At that moment, they heard a faint hiss as one of the airlocks in the corridor outside was opened.

"Quick!" said Melody and she and Xalata dived behind one of the consoles. "Do we do anything but keep hiding?"

"Quiet!" hissed Xalata. The two girls peered between the units and saw the door of the control room edge open slowly. A figure came in, dark clothes, hood over his head and the pair shrank away from their viewpoint so that there was little chance of being spotted. As they listened, quiet footsteps walked towards the main console and they heard a low whistle as the visitor discovered the controls.

"What in Jupes loops is this," whispered the voice and, as it did so, Melody and Xalata turned and stared at each other: "Glitch!" they mouthed and then both stood up suddenly and pointed at the startled figure.

Glitch bounced away from the controls and stumbled against a chair, sitting down heavily. "What the...!"

"Glitch! What are you doing here, you weasel!" screeched Xalata, dashing over to him with her fists clenched. "I've a good mind to remodel your face, your rotten little piece of space debris."

"Xalata! No!" cried Melody. "He can tell us what's going on. Can't you Glitch?" She turned to look at him and walked over, her eyes wide and a very no-nonsense look on her face. "Well?"

"Er, hi guys," Glitch said weakly, "Fancy seeing you here. Look, none of this is what it seems. I've been, er, stupid..."

"Nooo!" said Xalata, "who would have noticed? Why did you give me up to those two creeps, Fark and Machin?"

"Fark?"

"Yeah, Fark - you know, the guy in charge of security? He's running the show here and it's a bit of a horror story as far as we can see - and I don't know why, but you're tangled up in it."

"I didn't know it was Fark behind what happened - although I s'pose I should have joined the dots. I was told I had to get you to the Outpost for a lecture and then they would take care of things."

"Take *care* of things? What do you mean?"

"Not sure - I certainly didn't expect you to be grabbed like that, but thing was I'd been threatened."

"Oh yeah? What with?"

"That if I didn't do what they said, my sister back on Earth would get hurt. They had her captured and sent me a picture."

"And did they?"

"Did they what?"

"For Frank's sake, this is like pulling teeth. Have her captured?" Xalata was getting angry now...

"Er, no. Apparently not. The picture was a fake..."

"Well, yes. Of course. How dim are you?"

"Hmm. I think you're right. Pretty dim. I'm really sorry - I never meant to get you into this mess. Anyway, what *is* the mess?"

Melody stepped forward and put herself between Xalata and Glitch. "Look you two, let's put away our differences, huh? The fact is that there's something bad going down and we're here and could potentially stop it. Glitch, you've been an idiot but, well, you're here now and ... wait a minute. How the freak did you get here?"

"Wondered whether you might ask that. There's this portal, see? And it flips you from one side of the Moon to the other. I followed Fark into it - it's where you were grabbed Xalata - and then I found a truck and drove here. It was cool."

"Idiot! How can it be cool being such a dustbrain as you?" said Xalata. "Still, you made it and now you can help us sort things out."

"OK - that sounds like a plan. By the way, I saw that thing that destroyed parts of Habitat 14."

"The Cryomorph? It nearly had us, then we discovered that it doesn't go into some areas and we know why."

"Yeah, me too. I didn't go near it. Just let it amble off, but here's the thing, it's controlled. There's an antenna on its back along with an inset control panel."

The two girls looked astonished. "Really?" said Melody, "So someone's making it do the things it's doing. But who - Fark? And why?"

"Who knows," said Glitch, "But it's a sure thing that it's not a nice beastie to come across in a dark corridor. It would make tofu out of you."

"All right - enough talk. The thing we have to deal with is on that screen and we need to do something now..." As Xalata said these words the sound of the airlock hissing again reached their ears. They all glanced at each other and then, as one, dived for cover.

The door opened swiftly and into the control room walked Wiglet. He went straight to the control panel, touched a few items, frowned and then walked out once more. The airlock door hissed shut.

Chapter Thirty-three

Brett had lost no time in making his way across the LunarBase to the Outpost. As Fark had rightly concluded, Brett had soon decoded the passkey to the portal and, as he strode into the Outpost, his mind was on Xalata and Melody and where he would find them.

He found the cupboard once again and stepped inside, unable to see anything in the gloom and leaving the door ajar so that he could see what he was doing. However, Fark's notes had alerted him to where the control was and he bent down and touched the panel, making it glow. With a swift movement, he keyed in the code and a dazzling light heralded the opening of the portal.

With his heart in his mouth, he stepped through and into Habitat 14 - scene of so much destruction, as he remembered the news segment he had seen. Sure enough, there were the blasted walls, gaping holes visible in sections outside the airlocks that protected him from the vacuum of space. He moved forward, cautious and wary of any danger. There seemed to be no sign of people at all, although there were tracks on the floor - a combination of wheel tracks from the lunar carts that were used as trucks throughout the habitats, footprints of other people and prints of some creature that was not known to him - large almost circular pads that were printed in the dust, marking out a trail.

Brett decided to follow the wheel tracks, as he believed that he would need transport if he were to explore this forbidding environment. Down the long corridor he went, following footprints made by Glitch, unknown to him, leading towards a gallery that glowed a little brighter than the surrounding gloom of emergency lighting. As he approached, the hair on the back of his neck prickled and he could feel it slowly standing on end. "Bizarre," he muttered to himself, "There's nothing to be afraid of here."

Despite himself though, he couldn't help but feel a primitive fear, as though there were some great danger lurking nearby. He stepped forward again, the light barely revealing any sign of life in the bleak environment. There was nothing moving, nothing living, as far as he could see, nothing to be afraid of. Or was there? A few more paces, hesitant now as he still felt the fear crawling through him. Was it just the darkness or could he really sense the fact that there was something threatening him?

Then his nose told him that something was different, changing. A strange odour, half animal, half industrial, touched his senses - there was something that disturbed the air nearby, making it move and bringing with it the smell of its own body. A small tremor rattled through the habitat and then another. Brett looked around wildly. Where was it? What was it? He turned to run back the way he had come and then, he saw it. The Cryomorph was standing, observing him - huge, dark and threatening, its tiny eyes glistened dully in the half-light and its mouth was opened in a bizarre imitation of a grin.

Brett knew he had moments to live - his brain raced, planning exits, defences and ways to hide himself from this monster that had come from who-knows-where? Behind him now was the dimly lit area from which the trucks obviously came. To left and right were corridors, but they led to damaged areas of the habitat that were even more unsafe than the area in which he stood. He glanced behind as if to run down to the trucks then, with a bound, he leapt towards the Cryomorph, which stood back a step as its slow brain registered an unusual activity - a threat!

As the Cryomorph stood back, Brett dashed to its left and ran down its flank, leaving the beast to find a way to turn around in order to pursue its quarry. Brett lost no time - he ran as hard as his legs would carry him, dashing through corridors, turning unexpectedly into side passages and then doubling back along parallel ones, in the hope that his rapid flight would not be detected by the huge beast that was obviously preparing to pursue him.

Then he saw it - an abandoned truck. It was standing where it had been left, near to a suite of homes that had long since been left by human inhabitants. The truck looked to have been parked here not particularly long ago as it was not covered in the thin layer of grime that coated every surface of the damaged habitats. Brett leapt into the driving seat, checked the controls and pressed the go pedal. Nothing happened - no juice? Nope - he'd not activated it in his haste. Switching on, he then tried the pedal again and, sure enough, the truck pulled smoothly and silently away from the habitat area and down the nearest passage.

As he steered, Brett tried to get his bearings. In his flight, he'd not kept track of where he was running and now, he wasn't sure whether he was heading towards the Cryomorph or away from it. Coming out into a wider corridor, he had the choice of a left or right turn. Tyre tracks ran down the middle of the passageway and also prints that he now knew were those of the beast. Still no clue as to which way to go, so he opted for left and pressed the pedal to move the truck away from the danger.

As he drove, the habitat corridors became less damaged and cleaner, meaning that the tracks in front of him were less clearly marked. Where was he going? He hadn't a clue. All he knew was that, somewhere in this god-forsaken place, was Xally and, probably, Melody. And he meant to find them.

Chapter Thirty-four

Fark was furious. Tied up and not able to move, he seethed and ranted to an invisible audience. The gaffer tape bound him tight and although he struggled hard, he couldn't shift it or make any inroad into releasing a hand or a foot. As he swung himself around, the chair tilted precariously and he nearly lost his balance. Then, with another violent jerk, he tried to pull his right hand free, swinging his body to give him leverage. The chair tilted onto two legs and, then, Fark gave another twist and it was over, the chair taking its occupant to the ground with a crunch. There was a sound of snapping plastic and Fark suddenly realised that the arm to which his right hand had been tied had come away from the chair with the impact.

His arm was free, but he was still securely fastened to the other arm and both legs with lengths of the strong, sticky tape. He twisted around so that his free hand could pick at the tape on his other arm and, within a few minutes both hands were free.

Rapidly he worked on his two legs, pulling off the tape and rubbing feeling back into the limbs. "Tie me up would you, Mr Orbit? Is that what you'd do? Well I think there may be a new lesson on its way to you and it's one you won't want to learn."

He jumped to his feet, kicked the remains of the chair and tape to one side and then ran to the airlock door and let himself out. At speed, he headed for the TransTrak to the Outpost and then dashed to the cupboard where the portal was hidden. To his surprise the door was standing half open, but there was no sign of anyone inside. *Must have left it like that when I came back,* he surmised.

One thing was certain, Brett Orbit would be ahead of him. He'd have downloaded the access to the portal from his pad and would now be trying to be the hero. *Big surprise, Mr Orbit. Just you wait.* As he stepped inside, he pulled out a small control unit and touched some areas of its surface. *See what you make of this, you meddling creep!*

With a quick movement, he closed the door behind him, touched the small control panel near the floor, entered the passkey and then stepped into the portal that opened before him in a blaze of light.

Chapter Thirty-five

"What the...!"

"I can't believe it...!"

"For Frank's sake...!"

The three friends were astounded by what they'd just seen and as one, exclaimed their astonishment. Wiglet had walked in, reviewed the control panel and walked out and they couldn't believe that he was part of the plot to send the asteroid crashing to Earth, destroying Beijing and plunging Earth into a nuclear winter.

"Wiglet! He's the mastermind behind this plot!" Melody was beside herself with anger. "I just can't believe that he would do something like this and ... that means he's in league with Fark and Machin too! He's probably an Asttarian - this just gets worse. What shall we do? What *can* we do?"

Glitch had been looking thoughtful and he suddenly looked up and said, "We need to get that asteroid back on track or at least stop the override that has been put on it by Wiglet and his wicked friends."

"Oh yeah, brains? And how are we to do that?" Xalata's scornful answer made Glitch swing round and face her.

"Look, Xalata, I'm sorry 'n' all for what happened, but it wasn't meant. I was trying to look after my own and now we're all stuck in this together - so back off!"

Xalata looked angry and then she glanced at Melody, saw her pleading eyes and then looked back to Glitch. "OK. Yeah, you're right. It made me so mad that you had given me up to those creeps but I can see why. So now, we need to get out of this mess and find a way to stop the asteroid. Let's take another look at those controls and see what we can make of them."

Melody smiled and Glitch grinned, "Cool. Let's go save the world, huh? Always saw myself in that way."

"Glitch, you're a joke!" Xalata laughed. They all pulled themselves out from their hiding place and dashed over to the control screen. "So, what can we do - I don't understand the controls, don't get what's going on and don't know how to make this thing stop."

"I think we can work it out," said Melody and she touched a part of the screen that brought up the view from the asteroid, with the Earth glowing brightly in front of it. "There's got to be a status panel that shows the situation with all the controls for the engines. There need to be navigation tools to show where it's going and how fast - my bet is that's the most important bit. And there has to be some way of communicating with the team on Earth that are driving this thing - or were until Wiglet took it out of their hands!"

As she said those words, they were shocked by a woman's voice that came from the control panel, "Status critical. Mission Hephaestus is out of control. Target vector unstable and intercepted. Overrides initiated but failed."

"What's all that mean?" said Glitch, staring at the panel.

"It means that the mission control is no longer in control," replied Melody. "Can we speak back to them?" She touched a microphone icon on the panel and said, "Mission control, can you hear me?"

There was a delay and then Mission Control responded, "Affirmative, hearing you clearly. Please identify yourself."

"Oh, er, hi! I'm Melody Fret and my friends Xalata Orbit and Glitch - er, Justin Shaw-Storey are here with me too."

Again a slight pause as the messages flashed across space and around the Moon. "How are you able to interface with the mission please? This is a classified and restricted data stream. From where are you speaking?"

"We're on the Moon - LunarBase, in Habitat 14. We've just discovered this control room and can see what's happening but don't know what to do."

"Melody, I am Colonel Thien Thi of the Mars Terraforming Project, working on Mission Hephaestus. You say you are aware of what's happening?"

"Yes, well sort of. We can see from these controls that the asteroid is being targeted onto Beijing and we're fairly certain that you don't want that!"

"Indeed not," replied Colonel Thi. She continued, "You are our feet on the ground in the rebel stronghold - are you also aware of the faction that is diverting this mission?"

"Well yes, we think so. We believe it's the same people who made the mess of Habitat 14 with the Cryomorph."

"You are in great danger, Melody. You and your friends can help us to stop this awful tragedy from happening, but you will put yourself in harm's way in doing so."

Xalata suddenly spoke up, "Look, Colonel Thi, we have been kidnapped, chased by the Cryomorph, locked up, escaped - I don't think much else is going to scare us. There are some very bad guys here and they seem to want to make things bad for everyone, but we can stop them."

Colonel Thi responded, "Be aware that you are up against very powerful forces. These people are fanatics, driven by religious zeal and the teachings of their spiritual leader. They believe they are fulfilling their destiny and that of the world by destroying the scientific endeavor of the space community."

"Yeah, we've encountered them already. Nasty bunch, but we can sort them out.'

"Very well," continued Colonel Thi, "Please assist me with the retargeting of the navigational instruments as we are locked out of the controls here on Earth. The rebels have locked us out of the controls. It's impossible for us to change the trajectory of the asteroid. You can do that, by ensuring we have the correct coordinates entered at your end."

Glitch spoke suddenly, his face looking puzzled. "Er, Colonel Thi. This is Glitch here - er, Justin Shaw-Storey. Could I ask you a quick question?"

Colonel Thi answered instantly, "Of course, Justin."

"OK," Glitch hesitated, "How did you know someone would respond to your distress message, here on the Moon?"

"Good question. We knew that there was a duplicate control room on the Moon and so we were hoping we could find someone just like you to help us make the control changes."

Glitch gestured to the others, waving frantically and sawing his hand across his throat as much as to say, *cut the link*. Xalata and Melody stared at him uncomprehendingly. "She answered too quickly," hissed Glitch in a tone that wouldn't be heard by the Colonel.

"What do you mean?" said Melody.

"I know," whispered Xalata, "Transmissions take time to cover the distance between Earth and the Moon. At first there was a pause between our messages and her replies. But then she forgot and replied to Glitch's question instantly! She's a fake. And she's here on the Moon!"

Chapter Thirty-six

"Don't be silly, Glitch," retorted Melody. "That's definitely Earthbase calling in. We can see what's happening. If it wasn't them calling, then who would it be? Wiglet, Fark and Machin don't need us to modify the controls - they could do it themselves. I believe her."

"But it was far too quick. Comms waves with conventional radio take about one and a half seconds to reach us from Earth. Then you have the relay time to this side of the Moon. She can't have answered me that quickly!"

"I think it was just a coincidence. She answered you before you'd finished speaking, that's all." Melody addressed the console again. "OK, Colonel Thi, we're ready to help you. What do we have to do?"

"Excellent," came the voice from the screen. "You've already identified the key elements of the console, I believe?"

"Yes, we have," replied Melody.

"Then please proceed as follows - we shall need to dig a little deeper into the source code of the controls to effect the changes we want to see. Please follow my instructions very carefully. Firstly, you'll need to find the Stage Instruction Array which is located to the left of your screen - when you open that, you'll need to use the following access codes..."

Colonel Thi continued with her instructions and Melody diligently followed them, watched over by Xalata and Glitch, who both interjected from time to time to ensure that she was making the right moves.

Glitch was still concerned. It bothered him that a technical fact was being overlooked, but now, consistently, there was a delay in the communications, as he had said there should be. Had he imagined the instant reply or had it just been a trick of his mind when under pressure?

As they worked, there were no signs of change of trajectory for the asteroid on the console. Xalata suddenly said, "Why's nothing changing? We're making all the corrections that you are saying - not that we understand thom - and everything seems to be exactly the same."

"The changes only work very slowly. We are moving an asteroid, please remember, something that has a huge mass. The timings are critical if we are to avoid it being grabbed by Earth's gravitational pull so we are now programming the fusion drive to take it back onto a path that will loop it around the Earth and then hurl it back towards Mars to pick up its original course."

"OK, I understand, I think. It just seems bizarre that we're making all these edits to the control code and can't see any sign of it on the meters here."

"The telemetry takes time to catch up, don't forget - what you are seeing is what happened some minutes earlier. There is a delay for the instructions reaching the asteroid and then there is a further delay for us to be able to receive the data that shows things are going to plan."

"Oh yeah, I guess so - hadn't thought of that," said Xalata. "So how long will it take for the asteroid to be back on track?"

"According to my calculations, it will be two days and thirteen hours and some minutes," responded the Colonel, "Now I believe..."

As she started to speak, there was the sound of the airlock and footsteps rapidly approaching. The friends had no time to hide and stared behind them in horror as the door opened and a very angry Wiglet marched in. He was holding some sort of weapon in his hands and he waved it at them, "You evil little traitors, all of you. How could you?"

Melody froze with terror but Xalata was up and at him in an instant. "Don't threaten us – we're stopping you from wiping out life on Earth. Who's the 'evil little traitor' now?"

 "Stupid girl – get out of my way. You're in league with them – why are you helping them?"

 "Helping who – you've set this up. You're behind this asteroid strike on Earth."

 "What? WHAT? What are you talking about? I've just seen the targeting on the screen, gone to get my calculations and was coming back to stop it," said Wiglet. "I walk in here and see you chatting with goodness knows who about retargeting the asteroid to strike the Earth..."

"We were stopping it, for Frank's sake! We could see from the controls that the asteroid was on course towards Beijing and, as we looked at it, Colonel Thi from the Mars Terraforming Project came on the line and asked us to take over the controls because they're locked out of them down on Earth."

"Colonel Thi? There is no Colonel Thi on that project. I should know, I'm one of the leads in the whole enterprise. You've been fooled and now we need to put things right. Get out of my way!" Wiglet was red with anger and Xalata, Melody and Glitch stood there with shock written across their faces.

"But we..." began Xalata...

"Great job, Wiggins, but I am pleased to say that this little girl 'ere...", a rough voice from the shadows echoed around the space, a voice that Xalata recognised from when she had been captured! "This little girl 'ere..."

"What? Who's little? Screw you!", shouted Xalata, leaping from the chair where she had sat, stunned by Wiglet's story. "Where are you, you worm?"

"This little girl 'as just assisted me in making the final adjustments to the asteroid's trajectory and shortly, the Earth is going to 'ave a very big surprise."

"Not so much of a surprise – they know it's coming," shouted Xalata. "We've been in contact with them and we've helped to change the trajectory back."

"I think not – you're forgetting, that was us 'helping' you." Fark stepped into the light.

"But your voice is different ..." said Xalata.

"Do you really think anyone talks like this," said Fark in his oily voice. "Nah, of course not," he returned to the rough tones once more. "That's my voice for greasin' around the likes of your dim father and her dimmer mother," he said as he pointed first at Xalata and then at Melody. "The real me is what you see - lovely ain't I? Now, let's just sort a few things out. Wiggins, put down your scanner - the kids'll think it's some sort of weapon!" He grinned and motioned for the group of them to move across the room, into a corner. "That's better, now I can keep an eye on the lot of you."

At that moment, Castrana Machin walked into the control room. She looked haughty and contemptuous and she laughed as she looked at the two girls and Glitch. "Colonel Thi from the Mars Terraforming Project here!" she mimicked and then laughed again at her own joke. "You must be really dense not to have realised it was someone on the Moon talking to you."

"Actually, we did realise..." said Glitch, "You missed the delay out of your responses a couple of times - only we couldn't quite believe anyone would be that crooked."

Castrana Machin laughed once more, "Crooked? Just taking you for a ride, my little cherub. What a pity, quite cute but no brain!"

Wiglet was looking furious. "Well, well. Castrana Machin, I do declare," he said, "I heard you were on LunarBase and assumed you'd be spreading your usual brand of idiocy. And I don't know what your involvement is here, Adolf, but these girls have been tampering with exceedingly delicate equipment that is controlling a mission-critical system for terraforming on Mars. I'm involved in the project from a strategic point of view and I came here as a result of information from my colleagues at the Mission Control. This Control Room is a secure and restricted area and I find it beyond belief that you are all in here."

"'Beyond belief' eh, Wiglet?" said Fark, "What's 'beyond belief' is that it took you cuckoos so long to catch on to what we were doing! Now, enough of the backchat. We need to get this lot locked away before any other meddlers come along and try to spoil the show."

"Oh I don't know," responded Castrana, "these kids were quite handy for making the final adjustments to fine tune the impact on Beijing. Thank you so much, my sweets! But now, as my lovely Mr Fark says, we need to put you somewhere out of harm's way."

Wiglet stood forward and faced Fark and Castrana, " I'm surprised Castrana, that you have graduated to this level of criminality. You can't really be doing this, surely? Millions will die. The Earth will plunge back into the Dark Ages and all the learning and advancement that has happened over the past millennia will just disappear."

"Exactly, my dear Wiggins!" oozed Fark, his old voice put on for effect. "The Earth and its inhabitants are an abomination - they're a virus on the face of a once beautiful creation and the Lord Asttar has spoken and wants to remove that abomination, keeping only his pure kin close to him."

Xalata suddenly burst out laughing, "Oh sorry - oops. I mean, *really*? 'Pure kin'? That's *you lot* of scheming scumbags? Are you serious?" She laughed out loud again and Melody looked at her with a worried face.

"Xalata. Shut up. They'll hurt us."

"They won't hurt us. They're weasels. Their stupid little ideas can't be part of the life we live, surely. I mean, really, can you take it seriously? 'The Lord Asttar'? Who the freak *is he,* anyway?"

"Oh you shall know him, my dear," said Fark, his eyes bright with the sparks of self-righteousness. "He's the Lord of Creation, the Master of the World and he will have his vengeance on those who speak ill of him."

"Bollocks!" There was a stunned silence.

"What did you say?" asked Fark.

"I think you heard me clearly, *Mister* Fark. I said 'bollocks'. It's an Anglo-Saxon word with a great etymology, actually. I read all about it the other day. It basically means, in the context I have just used it, 'nonsense'. What you are saying is medieval, superstitious nonsense that has no place in a race of people that is developing and the word I have just used sums it up pretty well, I think."

Melody simply stared at Xalata, while Glitch stood with his mouth open. Fark looked annoyed and then the oily smile crept across his face. "You'll get what's coming to you girlie, be sure of that. Now, let's go - back to where you came from, but this time I think we shall be a little more careful how we lock you away!"

With that, Fark pulled an EDW from his pocket - a small, but very effective Electrical Discharge Weapon that can disable people and does not risk damaging fragile environments such as those found on the LunarBase. "If I have to use this, I'm quite happy to do so. It won't kill you but, if it hits you, you'll wish it *had* killed you. So, let's go for a little amble back to the home you came from." He waved the EDW and the group walked back towards the outer airlock, Castrana Machin at the front and Fark bringing up the rear.

"You won't get away with this, Fark!" spluttered Wiglet.

"Oh, don't be so melodramatic my dear Wiglet," replied Fark in his old voice. "You know that I shall get away with this and that you will simply be a victim of the fall-out from the whole episode. It will be so gratifying to watch. Now, walk on!"

Chapter Thirty-seven

The home was as they had left it when they broke out from their improvised prison. Fark glanced around and, poking his head into the bedroom, spotted the dummy that was pretending to be Xalata. "Very clever. Quite a good likeness, my dear - particularly the 'air." Xalata glowered at him but said nothing, as Fark checked around the rooms to ensure that everything was it should be.

Castrana Machin simply stood and watched the four prisoners who had sat on the available seats in the living space. "You'll be quite comfortable here until our work is complete," she laughed. "There is food, water and even entertainment," and she pointed to the screen on the wall. "You're short of nothing you could possibly need - oh, except your freedom of course!" She laughed again and, as Fark emerged from the lobby she said, "And now we really must dash. So sorry to have to spoil the party."

They took a final look around the living area and then closed the door behind them. The outer airlock hissed and the four captives were left alone. They sat in silence for a few moments, considering their situation. Wiglet was the first to speak. "I'm baffled by a number of things, not least of which is how you come to be here."

"Yeah, well, we're baffled too, Mr Wiggins, if you don't mind me saying," said Xalata "What are you doing here and why did you tamper with the controls for the asteroid? Looks pretty suspicious to me."

"Your suspicions are unfounded, Xalata. The very fact that I am a captive too should inform you that my intentions are not the same as those of the people who just left. I am part of the asteroid programme for the Mars Project and I had received notice from Earth that another control had taken over from the Beijing base, locking them out. I knew that there had been another control room on Farside so I came to check."

"OK - I believe that," said Melody, "But how can you be here? We're on the other side of the Moon from the LunarBase and our homes. We got here through some sort of gateway that we discovered after Xalata was captured, but how do you know about it?"

"I too have a portal access, in the Academy," said Wiglet. "Portals are exceptionally dangerous, except under very controlled circumstances. However, I needed to use it in order to come to this control room and find out how it had been hijacked after I was notified by Beijing that the mission had been compromised. My task was to discover who was now controlling the asteroid. Imagine my consternation when I arrived back there and found that it appeared to be you! Now, of course, I realise that you were being tricked too and that you were genuinely trying to help."

"Yes we were and the problem is now that none of us can do anything about this situation because they've locked us in here," said Melody, her face showing her anxiety. "How ever shall we get out of here? What can we do?"

"We'll get them when they come back," said Xalata, "Jump 'em and beat their heads with the pans from the kitchen."

"That'll be too late ... they'll already have done what they intend to do. It's a disaster," wailed Melody.

"Oh, get a grip girl," snapped Xalata, "tears won't fix this. Now, let's think!"

While this exchange was going on, Glitch was sitting, facing away from the group and saying nothing. His brow was furrowed in thought and he muttered silently to himself as if he was working out a problem. After a few minutes, he stopped and turned around, "I may have an idea that will help us," he said.

* * * * *

Brett drove for what seemed like hours, but was actually only about 30 minutes. The truck was not very fast and he could see from the gauges that there was only enough power for about another 30 minutes. Then he'd have to go on foot, through passages and areas of the habitat that he did not know. Although all habitats were built on the same model, when you found yourself suddenly in a particular location, it was hard to know where you were actually going. Much of the place was unlit or only dimly so, with emergency lighting giving only the faintest glow to guide him where the corridors went.

He still worried that the Cryomorph would be pursuing him, but as far as he could tell, he had left it behind, in the dust - literally. He wasn't going to take any chances though and so he proceeded with caution, checking junctions between corridors and looking behind him regularly in case the beast were to be thundering up in his wake.

* * * * *

Castrana and Fark headed back to the control room, confident that their prisoners were safely locked away. This was to be the endgame of their plan and they didn't want it spoiled by a band of interlopers who didn't share their beliefs.

They opened up the airlock and went inside. The screens were still displaying the same instrumentation as before. Castrana touched one section and a view of the Beijing control room filled the screen. There was evident panic as people dashed around, worked feverishly at their workstations or consulted earnestly with each other. Control had been wrested from their hands and they could see the telemetry for the asteroid - it was heading straight for them! Castrana laughed quietly, "Fools! They'll be destroyed - all because of their arrogance. They have hours to live and there's nothing they can do because they are totally locked out of the controlling networks. No one can stop the Lord Asttar's will from being done!"

Fark smiled, "Yeah. We shall be celebrated throughout the universe as the ones who kept the faith, kept the Word and fulfilled our Destiny as the Lord Asttar's 'umble servants." He addressed another part of the main control screen and brought up the status screens for the asteroid's trajectory, engines and power readouts. "All systems nominal, Captain," he grinned. "Always wanted to say that. Now, let's make them final adjustments and then lock this sucker down."

The two of them worked for several minutes, double-checking their figures, monitoring the readouts and ensuring that everything was functioning to perfection. Then Fark said, "We're there - 'ere are the keys," and he produced two thin, transparent slivers of plastic that were marked with complex circuitry. "One for you. One for me. Now, insert your key, Castrana. Thank you. Now on my mark, let's perform the locking sequence." The two conspirators then twisted the keys in unison, pressed two sets of buttons on a console in front of the screen and then finally removed the keys.

Castrana put hers into a small pocket in her jumpsuit and Fark did likewise, sealing the pockets and ensuring that their keys were safe from harm.

"I think our work is complete," said Fark and Castrana beamed with pleasure.

"It certainly is, Adolf. I shall return to Nearside and prepare to watch the show. According to my calculations, we should be able to see the Earth impact from our observatory."

"Very good, Castrana. I shall join you directly, but meanwhile, I 'ave a little problem to take care of." As Castrana left, he stepped out of the Control Room into the atrium beyond and reached up to remove the protective strip from the area above the airlock door.

Then he pulled out his pad and navigated to an interface that monitored some remote activity. He touched a few controls and a scene came to life - movement down a corridor, swaying from side to side, the sounds of a beast in motion and a searchlight beam scanning for infrared, picking out hotspots of features ahead. And there, in the centre of the screen, was the clearly defined image of a truck in motion and, on it, a figure. Quite clearly, it was Brett. Fark touched some more controls and the image lurched as the creature gathered pace; a further touch and a blast of power erupted from the bottom of the screen as the huge Cryomorph discharged its lightning bolts into the wall ahead, blasting through into the corridor where Brett's vehicle had just passed.

*   *   *   *   *

"What is it, Glitch? What's your idea?" Xalata and Melody walked over to him while Wiglet stood to one side, looking sceptical.

"I'm not sure, but I think those guys were a bit crazy leaving us in here with the screen."

"How do you mean?" asked Melody.

"Well, I'm a bit nifty in the systems and coding department and I think - only think mind you - that we could hack into the door system through the screen there."

"What are you waiting for, Glitch. Do it. What do you need from us?" said Xalata, getting suddenly interested.

"Nothing really at the moment, but I think I could do with a drink."

"Oh yeah? They're over there, mate - help yourself. I'm still hurting from you giving me up to Fark and his crew."

Glitch looked a bit crestfallen. "Sorry, Xalata. Didn't mean to be pushy. You'll forgive me in time - probably about the same time I forgive myself." He walked over to the kitchen area, grabbed a drink and then sat back down, facing the screen. "I just need to get some interface access and I think we might have it." He pulled out his pad and then took his scanner and swept it across the screen on the wall. "Let's see what this tells us."

"Yeah, well," said Xalata, "you may have a problem there. The Q isn't showing up in here at all and you'll need that for your comms."

"Leave it to Mr Freeze, my lady," he responded with a grin. "I think I can certainly summon up a bit of connectivity - part of my ineffable skill."

"Hmm, you just can't 'f' it, can you," said Xalata with a little smile. She evidently liked Glitch, despite that fact that she was furious with him.

He worked for a few moments, creased his brow into a frown and then smiled. "Thought so. Here we go - I have connectivity and the public access and secure portals are mapped onto each other. If I can bridge that gap and jump into the secure area, we stand a chance of working out how to get that door open."

"Just a question," said Melody, "assuming we do get the door open and we can escape, what are we going to do? The Earth is in danger and those two creeps now have total control."

"I think," began Glitch, "that if I can control this portal, I may be able to hack across to the asteroid's control network too."

"Nonsense," said Wiglet, "that network is highly encrypted and coded. You'll not be able to get into it."

"You're quite right, Mr Wiggins, I won't be able to." The girls looked shocked. "But you may be able to. You have an access, don't you?"

"Yes, of course, but it's been blocked and I cannot now get into my workspace on there."

"You get me as far as the blockage, Mr Wiggins and I think I can do the rest."

Chapter Thirty-eight

The sudden terrible blast from behind him almost knocked Brett from the truck. The floor shook and the truck bounced, nearly hitting one wall, before righting itself and continuing straight down the corridor. As he looked behind, Brett saw the smoking hole in the wall, just where he had passed moments before and, as he watched, another blast hit the opposite side of the corridor as the Cryomorph demolished the wall in front of it. There was no time to lose; he hit the controls and the truck leapt forward again, just as the snout of the Cryomorph pushed through into the space behind him. It would be moments before it was in the tunnel with him and he had to get ahead if he was to stand a chance of survival.

How did it know that he was there? Could it see through the walls of the habitat? Evidently so ... and then Brett remembered the panel on the beast's back and the small antenna. It was being sent after him. *It's the hunter and I'm the prey*. The truck rounded a bend and came out into a small atrium area with three other tunnels leading away from the centre. Which to choose? There were no signs or labels indicating where the tunnels went - each one could be a dead end, leading simply to a cluster of homes. Others might lead on to the next section of the habitat, while others again might take him into industrial and research areas. A quick decision was needed. The ground vibrated beneath his feet as the Cryomorph thundered along the corridor behind him. It would only be a moment before it turned the corner and saw him.

On an impulse, he chose the left-hand turning and drove swiftly down it. He could hear the beast enter the space he had just left and then it stopped, reviewing its options and trying to make a decision about which way to go. Brett kept the truck going at full speed, desperately trying to build up a few minutes of distance between him and the certain destruction that lay in wait for him should he fail to escape the clutches of the Cryomorph.

*   *   *   *   *

Fark had left the Control Room and had grabbed his parked truck to head off back to the portal. With one eye on the route his truck was taking and the other on his pad, he was still watching the progress of the Cryomorph as it pursued Brett. *You'll not get away from me, you weasel!* he thought as he adjusted the beast's programme to blast through into the corridor where Brett was travelling. Although Brett could travel quickly through the habitat using the truck, the Cryomorph could cut off corners and short-circuit the process to ambush its prey when they least expected it.

He saw in a moment, that the beast had reached the atrium area and it was now clear he needed to choose the right path. Through the Cryomorph's eyes, he studied the ground, looking for the telltale tyre tracks that showed the route his intended victim had taken. The floor in that area was relatively clean and it took him a few moments before he spotted a mark leading into the left tunnel and he pointed the Cryomorph in that direction. *Hunt and destroy option initiated,* he thought as he touched a couple of pre-programmed controls.

*   *   *   *   *

The truck rolled on down the long corridor, passing other side openings. Brett had considered these but they were almost certainly homes that would be a dead-end trap for him, if he could not get inside to escape the beast. In any case, was there an escape? It could go where it wanted, blasting down walls and destroying the fabric of the habitat wherever it went.

A few moments later, he saw another atrium area ahead - larger this time, with more openings and a large doorway with an airlock that was standing partly open. *This is where I change trains,* he thought and he pulled alongside the entrance and leapt off the truck. As he did so, the Cryomorph hove into sight behind him, running at speed, shaking the ground and obviously preparing to blast him. Brett ducked into the doorway, closed the airlock and waited for the inevitable flash and noise that signalled a destructive bolt from the Cryomorph's charged weapons.

Nothing happened.

There was silence and Brett moved to the viewport to check out what was happening. The Cryomorph was standing still, facing the entrance, unmoving and apparently with no intent to attack. "What in Jupe's Loops is going on here?" he said out loud.

"Simple. It can't come past the secure zone."

Brett turned and saw Castrana. "You!"

"Hi, Brett."

*   *   *   *   *

"Let's work on the door first," said Melody, "then we can be doing other stuff while you hack into the controls for the asteroid."

"Sure thing," said Glitch, poring over his pad. On the screen in front of him a number of elements appeared that contained code and schematics of the habitat layout. "Just need to isolate where we are, first of all. So this is Segment 6 of Habitat 14 - is that right?"

"How would we know?" said Xalata, "we've been kidnapped, chased, imprisoned and escaped only to get locked up again. I wasn't really paying attention to the geography, Glitch!"

"OK, let's geolocate..."

"You don't need to, young man," said Wiglet. "It says where we are on the wall in the entry. Just go and check that, then we're not sending out unneeded transmissions from here. Keeping our profile low seems to me a good bet."

"Of course - knew I'd seen it somewhere," said Melody and she dashed out to the lobby and came back with, "Segment 6, Home 141, Habitat 14."

"Great - let's find this home's circuitry ... aha, here it is. Now, what are the pathways for the data systems ... here and here, I think. No, *here*. That's it. Now, let's see what levels of security the planners of this place put to protect their investment - not much, I'll bet."

He fiddled and grunted, peered and poked at his pad, muttering numbers and references, before finally declaring, "I think we're there," and triumphantly pressed an execute command on his pad. Nothing. "Right, that must be because..." he continued muttering to himself.

Melody looked at Xalata, "Another fine mess we've gotten ourselves into."

"Don't be glum," Xalata replied, "Wonder Boy over there will come up with something, maybe. Or maybe not, in which case it'll be down to you and me kid."

"I thought we were really kicking the bad guys, when actually, what we were doing was playing straight into their hands. I wish we'd listened to Glitch when he was saying about the time lag..."

"But we didn't, so there's nothing you can do. C'mon, look forward and not back. You can't change history, so you plan for the future. That's why I came to the Moon, after my aunt said much about those very words to me. We've got to hang in there and make sure the bad guys don't win. That creep, Fark!"

"I never liked him," said Melody, brightening a little, "He always makes my skin crawl and I can't stand his voice - although his new one is not much better. And what about Castrana Machin? I thought she was some hot-shot intellectual. Turns out she's as bad as the rest!"

"I didn't like her either," replied Xalata, watching Glitch as he programmed, "she's in Fark's thrall as far as I can see and ... hang on a minute Glitch, you're missing something." She dashed over to where Glitch was programming. "Look at the screen here and not just at your pad. What did you just do?"

"Erm, I don't know..."

"Go back a couple of steps to before I shouted at you."

"Normal state of affairs with you..."

Xalata clipped him around the head, gently. "Just do as I say and stop arguing - you know there's no point."

"OK - here we are - I had just entered the schematic of the main system when..."

"Yes, there - what's that?" Xalata pointed to the large screen. "If I'm not much mistaken, it's a standard secure access point. They're used everywhere in systems like this."

"What? How do you know that?"

"Why? What, with me just being a little girlie 'n' all?" she moved to clip his head again, but Glitch ducked and the swipe missed. "I'll get you next time, dullard! Meanwhile, get this freakin' door open..."

Moments later, there was a click and the airlock hissed gently.

"See, just needs a girl's direction, I think you'll find."

*   *   *   *   *

"What the..." Brett spluttered, "I can't believe you are here. What are you *doing* here?"

"I could ask the same of you, my dear Brett," Castrana replied smoothly. "I'm supposed to be here. What's your excuse?"

"Don't you 'dear Brett' me, you evil harpie. The best thing I ever did was getting away from you!"

"Ah memories ... so romantic. But then you always were a guy with simple pleasures, weren't you Brett? Little loved-up Brett. What a sweetie."

"I'm not rising to your bait, Castrana. You were a disaster from the moment we got together and I should have realised and run at that point..."

"Ah, but you didn't, you poor, love-sick child. So you hung in there, even though I gave you such a hard time. And then there was the child - ugh!" Castrana visibly shuddered as she spoke, "that little brat and, wonder of wonders, here she is on the Moon, with us. Happy family time!"

"You keep away from her, Castrana ... but ... oh glory, you're mixed up in this mess aren't you? Are you in with Fark and his ridiculous Asttarians?"

"Adolf is a lovely, lovely man, once you get to know him. He has the guts to do things that creeps like you wouldn't even think of. He has ambition - he's looking to..."

"...rule the world?", interjected Brett. "Don't make me laugh. That odious little rat couldn't rule a straight line."

"Oh, you'll see soon enough, what Adolf can do. He and I have just finalised our little plan and we're going to sit and watch the last act - the final curtain of our dramatic presentation. A demonstration to the perverted people of planet Earth that they cannot defy the will of our Lord Asttar..."

"Have you heard yourself? You sound just like that idiot, Frank Wordsmith."

"That is because he is leading us in the way of truth..."

"The way of truth? And what is your 'little plan'?"

"You'll see soon enough, Brett. Why don't you run along and find our unpleasant daughter?"

"Now why would I do that, when you can take me to her?"

"Not a prayer, loser. Find her yourself."

Brett studied Castrana as she sneered at him. She had been a beautiful woman once, but now lines of anger and disdain had distorted her previously attractive features so that she had aged before her time. He felt sorry for her at first and then corrected himself - this woman who had once been his wife had no right to any sympathy. She had treated him like dirt and walked out on him and their young baby daughter. He'd been relieved at the time although conflicted because he was so strongly drawn to Castrana. In time though, his memory of her had faded and, when her name appeared on the lecture circuit or in newspapers, he could separate his former love from the person she had now become.

He wasn't going to try and grab hold of her to make her take him to Xalata - she would resist and probably refuse point blank - so he had to approach it in a different way. Then he had an idea.

*   *   *   *   *

The door had opened, but no one made a move. "OK, what next?" said Xalata. "We hacked it, now what do we do? Do we head back to LunarBase and inform the authorities or go back to the Control Room? Or will Cruella DeVille and the Poison Dwarf still be there?"

Melody laughed, "They weren't in the same movie, stupid!"

"Yeah but the description fits, doesn't it?"

Wiglet stood up and reviewed the little group. "I think we could be considerably more useful by staying here, actually..."

"In what way?" said Glitch, looking up from his pad.

"This young man has managed to hack into a highly secure system that protects our environment..."

"Not just him, Mr Wiggins..." said Xalata.

"No, Xalata, quite correct. You as well. So with this combined brain power and my understanding of the asteroid mission, perhaps we can save the day after all."

"You mean hack into the controls?" said Glitch.

"Yes, of course. Why not?"

"Cool. Very cool. Whoa! Let Mr Freeze get his hands on it." Glitch was by now getting very excited. "Where do we start, what's the primary access?"

"Ah, there's the problem," said Wiglet, "I'm not sure. The entry point has always been restricted to a number of specific, identifiable devices."

"You mean, it will only work on those terminals and no others? We're doomed."

"Well yes, we would be, if it were not for the fact that I have one of them with me."

Glitch let out a yell of triumph and Wiglet pulled a pad from his pocket. Smaller than the others carried by the rest of the group, this one was evidently high quality and high technology. "Then it's easy," said Glitch, "we just..."

"Dim brain," said Xalata. "Whoever's controlling this will know about the other access points and will be monitoring them. If we just bowl in and access the system, they'll be on to us in a flash."

"Exactly, Xalata," said Wiglet. "So we need to mask our presence - something I suspect you are quite used to doing, Justin."

"I don't know what to say, Mr Wiggins," replied Glitch, looking sheepish, "I would never..."

"Never mind the excuses - just remember that we at the Academy know an awful lot about what goes on. We may have taught you everything you know, but we've not taught you everything *we* know! Now, first, set up one of your cloaks to get us onto the system unseen..."

*   *   *   *   *

Fark had headed off at high speed to get back to the portal so that he could enjoy the spectacle of the asteroid's impact at leisure in the surroundings of his own home. It was going to be wonderful, watching one of the most momentous events in Earth's history since the dinosaur extinction. This time, it would be the extinction of mankind on Earth and then he and his fellow Asttarians could return to a clean planet, wiped clear of the virus that had infected it and that threatened to infect the rest of the solar system - people!

His truck bowled along the corridors and he avoided debris from where the Cryomorph had blasted through walls as he navigated to the portal point. He was excited by what had happened and the way in which they had handled the two girls and the boy. They were well out of harm's way now!

The truck slowed around the bend and there, in front of him, was the atrium area where the portal always revealed itself to transport him back to the Outpost. He stepped down from the truck and pulled the control from his pocket, activating the circuitry that would open the portal. Except that this time, it didn't. There was no sign of the portal and no matter how he signalled for it to appear, it stubbornly refused to do so.

He punched codes into the device, checked its power levels, sought out the receiver plate that was embedded in the wall of the habitat, high up and out of reach, then used the control near to the plate, hoping against hope that the portal would reveal and he could step through, leaving the wrecked habitat behind him. Frustrated now, he was tempted to fling the control across the atrium space, but he restrained himself, uttering a quiet "Aaaagh!" as he realised that his way back was compromised.

What was he doing wrong? There had been no problems previously, even though this was a restricted technology that few people were licensed to use. He knew it was dangerous and also knew that failsafes within the system would lock out any user if there were the slightest chance that an error would occur.

He desperately wanted to see the destruction of Beijing and, ultimately of all mankind on Earth, but here he was, stuck Farside and unable to get back to the comfort of his home. Of course, his pad could give him all the access he needed, but he felt vulnerable here. The Cryomorph was still lurking in the dark corridors and Fark was unsure whether the little control he had over it would extend to protecting himself from its built-in destruct cycle that triggered when it saw human forms.

He made a decision. Stepping back onto the truck, he spun the wheel and sent it back the way he had come, transporting him in the direction of the Control Centre.

*   *   *   *   *

Brett stood and studied Castrana. He thought he knew how he would get to her and persuade her to take him to Xalata. She stared straight back at him and said, "You have no reason to be here, Brett. This area is restricted and you don't have clearance."

"Ah, but I do," he replied. "I'm senior in the Lunar Hydroponics division and that gives me access to pretty much any laboratory, either Nearside or Farside."

"Not this one, it's out of bounds."

"Oh, and how will you stop me seeing what's here? Is this where you're hiding Xalata?"

"No, she's safe in the ... ah! Thought you'd catch me? I'm not falling for simple mind games from an idiot you like you. Now leave the premises!"

"Nope - in fact, I'm going on walkabout," and, with that, Brett pushed forward, past Castrana, who shouted and tried to pull him back. "Don't be crazy, Castrana. I'm twice your size and you can't stop me." He headed further into the building and spied the airlock into the Control Room. "See, there's always something interesting going on, on the Moon. What have we here?"

"It's none of your business," said Castrana, still vainly trying to stop him going into the room. "Stay out!"

"OK - I shall, on one condition?"

"What? What condition?"

"C'mon brain cell, I think you know what condition."

"Take you to the brat?"

"Indeed, otherwise, I'm going to poke around inside this place and find out exactly what you are up to here." *I shall do that anyway*, he thought darkly, *but you're too stupid to realise that.*

"OK. I'll take you there, but then you need to get out of here. It's not safe."

"Since when did you care about my safety, Castrana? Or any one else's for that matter. Come on, let's go." And Brett led the way out of the Control Room and back into the atrium. Castrana followed behind, but Brett could tell that she was plotting something. "I think you can drive the truck and I'll just keep my eye on what you are doing."

"Yeah, yeah," said Castrana wearily and she got into the driving seat while Brett wheeled around the back of the truck to take up his position next to her. He turned to face her. "Drive. Let's find our daughter."

"Whatever," replied Castrana as she swung the wheel and sent the truck humming down a corridor, back towards the home where Xalata and her friends were captive.

Chapter Thirty-nine

Back in their unsecured prison, Glitch, Xalata, Melody and Wiglet worked feverishly to access the controls of the asteroid. Glitch had cloaked their access to the system in a matter of a few moments, much to the astonishment not only of Wiglet and the girls, but also of himself. "Blimey, that's really weak! I can't believe that they have kept things so poorly protected."

"I think you are benefiting from the access route carved out by the people who have intercepted this mission, actually, Justin," said Wiglet.

"Look, Mr Wiggins, can I just say ... enough with the 'Justin', OK? I'm Glitch. Always have been and always will be."

"Yes, of course. I should have thought. Young people prefer their 'tags' don't they? So, er, Glitch. Let's get this asteroid back on track!" and with that, Wiglet used the access that had been made by Glitch and logged into the system with his own codes. "All seems to be OK. This will be the clincher though, when I go public through the portal."

"Everyone will know you are there?" asked Xalata, "So, the bad guys might try to stop you?"

"Yes indeed. However, I have a few tricks and I know my young friend here has some too," he nodded in Glitch's direction. "So, here it is ... and I'm in."

Melody peered over Wiglet's shoulder, "What's the status, Mr Wiggins?"

"On a quick glance, everything looks set on course for Earth. All course adjustments are complete and the system has been locked down."

"Locked?" said Melody, "But we can unlock it, can't we?"

"I believe so, given the level of access I have. However, we shall need to tread with caution as I don't want to set off any potential firewall bombs that might block us from access altogether. So we shall try a few little devices first ... Melody, my dear, I shall need your help please. Can you work out the navigation coordinates from the original target data and then provide me a course plotting beginning at, let's say, 20:30 GMT?"

"Sure thing, Mr Wiggins," said Melody. "Xalata, you can help me and check my pad's maths."

"Yep - OK, but maths and I live on different planets. You explain what you're doing and I'll sense check it. If I'm stuck, Glitch can help me out."

"As I see it, we have three choices," said Melody. "First, we take the current trajectory and bend it back on a continuous curve so that the asteroid will create a huge arc and miss the Earth by a big margin. The problem with this approach is that it's going to rely on the engines working flat out for a long period.

"Second, we simply divert the asteroid and make it plummet into the Sun. That's easy as far as it goes, but it will waste all the effort and money that's been put into the terraforming operation on Mars and it will mean that that project is put back for probably a couple of years.

"Third one - we tweak the current trajectory so that, instead of hitting the Earth, it swings around it and we slingshot it back to its original target on Mars."

"Sounds risky," murmured Xalata.

"Yep, but it's the simplest adjustment to make and doesn't rely on the fusion drives doing a huge amount of work. That's my best option, I believe."

"Gambling with the Earth, at all?"

"No - you have a better idea?"

"Nope."

"OK, then let's get calculating. First, I'll need the target impact area on Mars - you source those data for me while I work on the rest..."

The two girls grafted away at their calculations, while the others busied themselves with their own tasks.

Wiglet was already embedded in his work, staring intently at his pad as he produced a number of frames on the screen that contained elements on the navigation tools. "Glitch, can we use the big screen to work together on this? I want to bring together my interface from the pad along with Melody's one to combine things together then we can have a good overview of what's going on."

"Sure thing, Mr W." said Glitch and he worked away at the screen and, borrowing Wiglet's pad for a moment, touched a few areas, entered a piece of code and moments later, the pad's contents appeared on the big screen. "There you go - and all interactive too," and Glitch stood and swept elements from Wiglet's pad across the screen.

Melody's hands flew across the screen. Streams of data merged beneath her fingers and Xalata stood with her, following her every move and watching the process as it developed.

Within ten minutes, the team had established the coordinates of the revised route, had determined where the asteroid stood and had laid down the process for making the course corrections that would prevent the giant rock from hurtling into the Earth.

"OK guys," said Xalata, "we're ready to upload the new instructions and to prime the system to accept our commands. Mr Wiggins, can you provide the necessary codes to unlock the main interface and then we can execute the code that Glitch has just written, assuming it works." She looked pointedly at Glitch.

"Course it'll work. Let me just check it once more though - put doubt in my mind, why don't you?"

"I'm getting to know you," said Xalata, "and I still don't trust you, so don't screw this up and then I might be more likely to look at you favourably!"

"Honoured, I'm sure," muttered Glitch.

"Ready Melody? Glitch? Mr Wiggins?" said Xalata, "cos now we're going in. Let's have the code for the main interface."

Wiglet touched his pad and found the interface. Then he entered a series of complex codes, touching the pad from time to time with a sliver of plastic that was evidently some type of biometric key. "That should do it," he said.

The team waited and saw to their horror that nothing was happening. "What's wrong?" said Melody.

"It's locked still," said Wiglet "It's not giving me an error. It's waiting for further input. There must be either another key needed or..."

"Or what," said Glitch, anxiously.

"Or, they've imposed a physical key requirement on the terminal at the Control Room. If that's the case, we'll need two physical keys, not dissimilar to this," - he waved the piece of plastic. "Without them, we cannot do anything and the asteroid will continue on its course. This key may work, in conjunction with another one, but we don't know where the keys are or even who the keyholders might be."

"I have a good idea who it'll be," said Melody, "Fark and Machin. Those two weasels will have set this up and we need to get the keys back from them. I'm going to the Control Room to find the key. If I can get it, then I'll contact you from there."

"You can't go on your own," said Xalata, "I'll come too."

"No, you need to stay here - the navigation will need to be adjusted as we have not been able to activate the change in the timeframe we set. New coordinates for the start point will need to be entered and the calculations will need to be run again. You and Glitch can sort that. Let me find the key!"

And with that, Melody dashed to the airlock, turned, waved and walked out.

"Fry that!" called Xalata. "Glitch - you're in charge of navigation," and she ran out of the door after Melody.

*   *   *   *   *

"Fret monster! Wait for me!" Xalata yelled as she ran after the fast-disappearing shape of Melody, across the atrium. Then suddenly, she realised that she ought to be quiet. She had no idea whether their captors were nearby or not, but there was no point in waking them up or disturbing them, whatever they were doing. And then there was the Cryomorph - who knew where that was?

She ran in the direction she thought took her to the Control Room, but suddenly realised that she had missed a turning somewhere. Melody was nowhere in sight and the only way out of the situation appeared to be to go back.

*   *   *   *   *

Melody ran as fast as she could go. Her feet pounded the dull white surface of the corridor as she navigated the route she knew, turning quickly around corners before arriving at the Control Room atrium. She had been certain that no one would be there, but, as she approached, she could see a truck standing abandoned in the area in front of the Control Room. She heard the hiss of the airlock opening and she darted behind a corridor opening and watched as two people emerged.

She nearly called out, for there was Brett - Xalata's Dad, walking with Castrana Machin. It didn't seem a very pally association though as Castrana was scowling with evident anger and Brett was gripping her arm as he guided her out of the door, obviously intent on ensuring that she didn't escape.

They headed off down the corridor that Melody had just left and, as they did so, Melody darted into the Control Room entrance and left the airlock door ajar. She didn't want to be trapped in there. She ran into the big operations room and searched the surfaces for any signs of a key. There appeared to be none, yet she found two slots in the interface unit that evidently took similar keys to the one that Wiglet had shown her and used himself.

Where could the keys be hidden? Then she realised. "Idiot!" Of course, the keys would be with the two people who had committed this crime and one of those had just left the building. She turned to run back the way she had come when the door opened and Fark walked in.

"You again?" he smiled. "Just what I need ... a hostage."

*   *   *   *   *

Brett and Castrana Machin marched out of the Control Room and headed back towards the home where Xalata and her team had been secured. Castrana's mind was working overtime, trying to think how she could get away from Brett, fool him and overpower him, but he was big, strong and angry and she was no match for him. She led the way sullenly, knowing that she was potentially incriminating herself, once Brett realised the extent of what she and Fark had done.

They walked in silence, passing through corridors and past installations that were part of the LunarBase infrastructure and eventually arrived at the atrium leading into the home where the captives were all held. "OK - that's my part of the deal. She's in there. Now let me go."

"If you think I'm just trusting your word, you're very mistaken Castrana. You've always been a slippery liar and I have no reason to think you've changed." Brett pushed her forward and they walked into the corridor where the entry to the home was situated.

"That's impossible. The door's open," gasped Castrana. "They were all locked in and secure."

"Maybe you've underestimated her - but you said 'they'. Who else was with Xalata?"

"A group of interfering brats and an old teacher. No one valuable."

"Castrana, you're a rat. You still amaze me with your callousness. Let's go in and see what's happened."

They pushed open the door and entered the lobby and were surprised to hear voices. As they went further in, they opened the access to the living space and there in front of them were Wiglet and Glitch, intently working at the large screen at the end of the room. They turned as the pair walked in.

"Brett, well done for finding us," Wiglet said. "I have no idea how you got here, but thanks for capturing this woman. She thought she had imprisoned us, but as you can see, we are free to do what we want! However, there's a crisis - the asteroid will impact Earth if we don't stop it and divert it back to its original track."

Brett looked horrified while Castrana simply smiled crookedly and said, "You'll not stop the will of the mighty Lord Asttar!"

"Oh please, can it with the Lord Asttar stuff. I find it hard to believe that a supposedly intelligent woman like you can be hooked in by this fairy-tale nonsense," said Brett. "It's insulting to the brain power of those people who have fought to make advances in the world to everyone's benefit."

"You're deluded, Brett. Anything you have, you have because Lord Asttar wills it. He gives and he takes away."

"Yeah, well I think we shall be taking away your liberty for a little while - do you think that your Lord Asttar has willed that too?"

"It's all part of his purpose..."

"Sure, you can never win these arguments. Let's get down to business. Xalata is not here, unless she's hiding in one of the other rooms?" said Brett.

"No Brett, she ran out after Melody. They're both heading for the Control Room and..."

"That's where we have come from," interrupted Brett anxiously. "We saw nothing of them."

"Maybe you missed them...?"

"Maybe the Lord Asttar had other plans for them?" said Castrana, slyly.

"Another word, Castrana and I shall not be responsible for my actions," Brett glared at her and she took a step back, afraid that he might strike her. "Do you really think I would hit you? Is that how you judge me to be? It doesn't matter how much I detest you, after all you've put me through, I could never bring myself to strike you or anyone else. After the first blow, the person who has dealt it has lost the argument."

"Very true," said Wiglet, "but none of this helps us to know where the two girls are."

"Er, guys," interjected Glitch, "we need that key and we need it now..." He pointed to the screen and the impact schedule showed they had only 24 hours left before the Earth was to be obliterated. "And there's worse news, I'm afraid. If we don't get this asteroid back on track in the next four hours, I've calculated that the gravitational pull will be too strong for the fusion drives to prevent the impact."

Chapter Forty

Xalata decided to retrace her steps, but she had dashed out in such a fluster that she had completely missed where she was in the habitat. The surroundings all looked identical and she knew that she needed to get back to where she started ... but which way was that? "For Frank's sake! How can you be so stupid?"

She turned around and walked back to the atrium she had just left. The signage didn't help - it simply told the numbers and directions for each of the habitat elements, but she had not registered which building they were in. She could spend hours trying to find it again. "I need to find the Control Room. I can make my way back from there. That's where Melody is in any case. So, which way?"

She chose a direction and set off, hoping to see something familiar, but the landmarks in the habitat were few and far between. Then, she suddenly came to her senses. "How thick? Speak to someone," and she pulled out her communicator. Accessing Melody's details she called through to her, but there was no response. The relays for comms seemed to be out - probably part of the destruction that had happened during the Cryomorph's rampage through the other end of the habitat. She tried Glitch - no result. Then her Dad - likewise. "OK, girl. You're on your own," and she continued walking.

*   *   *   *   *

Melody looked at Fark, open-mouthed. "I thought you had gone back to LunarBase!"

"Yeah, that 'ad been my plan, but now I seem to 'ave 'ad to change them. You'll be good insurance in case we meet Xalata's meddlesome father. I've some plans for him since he really was not very nice to me and I intend to give 'im a little repayment. Now, what are you doing 'ere and 'ow did you manage to get out of the locked 'ome I put you in?"

"You're not as clever as you think, Fark..."

"Mr Fark to you..."

"You've been outwitted, Fark and your plan will not succeed."

Fark's face looked like thunder. "What do you mean? You kids can't do anything and Wiggins is too stupid to know what to do."

"I think you may have miscalculated. We have control of the asteroid and it's not going to hit Earth any more."

"Impossible. The whole system is locked down. We have made it so no one, either here on the Moon or at the Mission Control in Beijing, can do a thing. The Earth is doomed."

"Wrong," said Melody. "You made a mistake. We got in."

"You can't have. It needs this key and another one before anyone can access the controls." He pulled the sliver of plastic from inside a pocket and pointed it at Melody. "You just can't do it."

Melody gasped in horror, looking wide-eyed with fear. Her face drained of colour and she looked as if she might keel over.

"Yeah, you might well look afraid, girlie. It's all doomed."

But Melody was not looking at him, not looking at the key, but directly behind Fark, with growing terror in her eyes. She pointed slowly and Fark realised that something was amiss. He turned his head to look and, as he did so, Melody snatched the key with her outstretched hand and dashed for the airlock door. Fark howled with rage as he felt the key leave his fingers and he ran after her and reached the airlock as it slammed shut and locked.

Melody, on the other side, knew that Fark would need to recall the code for the door and unlock it so she ran out into the atrium and then headed back in the direction of the home where the others were held. She had a good 30 seconds lead and she hoped against hope that she would be in a position to deal with Fark once he caught up with her.

*　　　*　　　*　　　*　　　*

As Xalata walked she kept thinking that the area she was entering looked familiar - and in a way, it was, in that everywhere looked the same. Then as she continued on, she would find the same blank corridors and then an atrium. She was hopelessly lost and yet knew she could not be far away from her starting point. In an active habitat, this would not have been a problem as she would have had waypoint guides that could indicate where the features were for each area, but these were remotely controlled and since the habitat had been abandoned, they were no longer operational.

Turning into yet another space, she suddenly spied something that could speed up her search - a truck. It sat, charging quietly, in a truck bay that was used normally by the maintenance teams who ran the habitat. Leaping forward, she jumped into the driving seat. The truck immediately woke up and was ready for action so she pressed the Go pedal and she was away, speeding through the white corridors. *I don't want to get back to the portal ... I need to find the Control Room, or the home where we all are being held,* she thought as she drove along. As she whizzed down yet another long white tunnel she had a feeling that the area ahead actually was familiar. There were some tracks in white dust where a truck had followed before and she recalled that she had seen something similar near the Control Room.

As she rounded another corner at speed she spied Melody dashing away across an atrium and as she approached, she saw Fark fling open the door of the Control Room and throw himself after Melody. Without missing a beat, Xalata pushed the truck even faster and drove straight at Fark who, seeing her hurtling towards him from the corner of his eye, dived to one side as she flashed past.

In a moment she was upon Melody and she shouted urgently, "Jump in. Jump IN!" and kept the truck rolling beside her. Melody looked amazed and then hopped neatly into the seat next to Xalata as the truck accelerated away back to the home.

In only a few moments, they swung in front of the entrance to the home and they leapt off the truck and in through the airlock door. In a flash, Melody locked the door and then reprogrammed the code so that no one outside could get in.

As they entered the living space they were amazed to see not only Glitch and Wiglet, as expected, but also Brett and Castrana Machin.

"Dad? How in Luna did you get here? And what's *she* doing here?", said Xalata, pointing at Castrana.

"Xally, thank goodness you're safe," said Brett as he ran to her and gave her a hug.

"Yeah, well OK Dad, that's enough OK?" said Xalata, hating the public display of affection.

"Sorry, Xally, but I was worried sick about you. Now I know what this one and her evil sidekick have been planning, I can't describe how relieved I am."

"OK guys, enough of the tearful reunions," said Melody. "Look what I have!" and she gleefully produced the plastic key.

Xalata looked stunned. "How did you get that?"

"Fark decided to make a generous donation to our Save the World campaign."

"What!" exploded Castrana, "He did *what?*"

"He gave me the key," responded Melody, "and so now we can make the corrections to the asteroid's trajectory."

"He's fast behind us," said Xalata, "but he won't get in because Melody's reprogrammed the door. So we can concentrate now on the job in hand. The question is, what do we do with this one?" and she pointed to Castrana.

"He *gave you* the key?" spluttered Castrana. "Why would he do that?"

"Well, it was not altogether willingly. Let's just say that I am a better actor than he is a reactor! Now, let's do it folks."

*   *   *   *   *

Outside the home, Fark tapped furiously on the entry pad, trying to sort out the new combination. Nothing worked. In frustration, he kicked the door, but to no avail. Then he sat on the truck that had been abandoned by Xalata and Melody and waited. He couldn't leave the area and all the protagonists were inside, no doubt finding a way to fox his plans. Then he remembered he was not alone. Off he went, in search of reinforcements.

Very quickly, he arrived at the area where he had left his small team. The two other guards had been working on packing equipment that had been used during their time in the habitat, but now it was time to move out.

"Change of plan, lads," said Fark. "For reasons I won't go into now, there's a situation in the lockup we used. I need to get back in there, but they've changed the code so that I can't get in. I need an alternative plan ... "

He stopped for a moment and realised that, by talking about it, he had spurred on his own ideas. "Wait, I have it!"

And without another word, he hurried out, back to the truck and pulled out the control unit that was hidden deep in his pocket. Driving back to the home, he hopped off the truck and removed the thin plastic device that kept the Cryomorph at bay.

"Oh yes, indeed. I have it!" And he started to adjust the controls.

*   *   *   *   *

"Never mind the tearful reunions," shouted Glitch, "we're up against time here! Let's have the key and make things jump back into place."

Melody handed over the sliver of plastic and Wiglet took it and paired it with his, engaging the two as part of a virtual key on the main screen. Each flashed in turn and circuitry inside them lit up to demonstrate that the encryption algorithms were being compared and unlocked.

"This will take a moment or two," said Wiglet, "and then we should have clear access through to the command system. My access on its own is insufficient. So now..." He stopped speaking and looked at the screen in dismay - an error message indicated that the two keys were incompatible.

Castrana Machin smiled to herself, but that look was seen by Xalata, who then dashed across the room and grabbed her by the arm. "You knew it would fail!" she shouted, "and you just stood there and let us do it. Don't you realise what you're doing here? The Earth will be destroyed and the people on it will all lose their lives. Is this what your wonderful religion is about - getting rid of everyone who doesn't agree with you?"

"You wouldn't understand, sweetie," said Castrana, "your little mind can't get around the concepts that the Lord Asttar deals with. His will is all that matters. His will directs what I do and all the others who follow him. His will is the Right Way." Her eyes were alight with religious fervour and her voice sounded strong in the room. Everyone watched her as she spoke and there was then a sudden silence.

Melody broke it. "There are two keys. Fark had one and therefore I think it's fairly logical to assume that you have the other since you and he were buddies in this little game. Hand it over." Melody moved closer to Castrana and stood next to Xalata, her hand outstretched and she stood in front of her waiting.

"Melody is of course correct," said Wiglet. "You are in no position to bargain or hold out on us, Ms Machin."

"Give it up, Castrana," said Brett, "because either you give us the key or we shall take it from you."

She stood there impassively, with her hands by her sides and a fixed expression on her face. "Touch me, Brett and you'll pay dearly for doing so. The Lord Asttar doesn't..." but she was unable to finish the sentence because Brett had leapt across the chair in front of him and grabbed Castrana's arms behind her, immobilising her.

"Girls, check her out please," he said while Castrana kicked and bucked and shouted.

"I'm not going near her while she's kicking like that," said Xalata, "and anyway, are we sure she has the key?"

"Yep," said Melody. "It's the only logical place for it to be. Fark wouldn't hold both. They will have been doing their evil deeds in the Control Room together, locked it up and gone their separate ways."

"You evil little cats," spat Castrana, "you'll regret this!" as Xalata moved towards her, coming at her from the side. "Have you told her yet, Brett? Our little secret?"

"What secret?" Xalata paused and looked at her father. He looked conflicted so she said again, "What secret, Dad?"

"Go on! Tell her," scoffed Castrana, "or shall I do it?"

"Tell me what?" Xalata was getting annoyed now. "Dad?"

"Well, Brett...?" grinned Castrana.

"You, be quiet. You're frying my wiring big style and I might do something that would get me in deep trouble, so, can it!" Xalata's face was determined and Castrana fell silent.

"You're not going to like this, Xally," said Brett, "But ultimately the truth would come out soon, I guess. I was going to tell you when you were a little older so that you'd understand the adult viewpoint."

"Oh please, you'll be telling me she's my mother next!" laughed Xalata.

"Yes, that's exactly what I have to tell you."

The room went silent. Xalata looked confused and then started to say, "But I thought..."

"Guys..." Glitch's voice broke the suspense. "Sorry to break up this reconciliation, but time's running out."

"Reconciliation? My arse!" shouted Xalata and she grabbed Castrana and roughly began to search her pockets. In a matter of moments she triumphantly produced the plastic key and waved it in front of Castrana's face. "More of this later, *Mummy*!" she yelled, "but for now, we've a world to save."

Chapter Forty-one

The Cryomorph didn't really sense anything, as it was largely a constructed creature that functioned on a very low level. Its aimless wanderings of the corridors and atriums of Habitat 14 were simply down to no received instructions. It was essentially a destruction machine; much like an excavator that is used to dig holes or a propulsion unit that is used to launch spacecraft, it had a function that was programmed by humans and it acted to those humans' commands, even if that meant the destruction of other humans.

It had been created in labs in the back end of Habitat 14, alone and as a huge experiment in the viability of something terrifyingly indestructible. It wasn't just that it could fire frighteningly powerful bolts of electrical discharge that blasted through the reinforced materials of the habitat - or send scalding streams of acid to burn through metals; it could also be programmed to find and hunt down a particular individual and destroy them in whatever way seemed sensible to its tiny brain.

So, when it received its instructions from Fark to attack the home where the team were fighting to redirect the asteroid, it simply obeyed and set off to the coordinates where its targets were working, lumbering along at a surprising speed from the place where its most recent wanderings had taken it. The ground shook as it stumped along on its short, stout legs, carrying a load of several tonnes of body mass that simply shrugged off every attempt to damage it.

Weapons would be useless; fire merely irritated it - it had met enough of that when it was destroying the further parts of the habitat; and the vacuum of space had not the slightest effect on it, meaning that it could blow open the seals of damaged areas and cross them, despite the dangers to normal life.

Its pace quickened as the signals that were guiding it urged it onwards to its target. And the target was completely unaware of the fact that it was approaching.

*   *   *   *   *

Meanwhile, Fark was busy removing the protective unit from the entrance to the home. The thin strip of plastic would deflect any attentions of the Cryomorph but, without it, the home was vulnerable. He grinned to himself. *Can't believe I didn't think of using the beast to get rid of them all. This will fix my little problem!*

He wasn't sure of the Cryomorph's location so had no idea how long it would take to arrive, but he had programmed it to arrive at the home, then blast the entry and kill the people inside the building. He, meanwhile, would be well out of the way, hiding behind another airlock that would protect him.

He checked that all was set and then he left the area, grabbing the truck that the girls had arrived on and driving back to the Control Centre in order to watch the final hours of the Earth.

*   *   *   *   *

Inside the habitat, Melody had decided to check the airlock codes were holding up and, as she studied the screen, the outside view showed Fark heading off on the truck. "Hey guys, something strange. Fark's been trying to get in but now he's going off - what do you think he's up to?"

There was no reply - everyone was intently working at his or her task to pull the asteroid back on course. Then Wiglet spoke up, "Melody, we really need your revised coordinates now. We're in the interface and we've unlocked the access to the navigation system. You were going to revise the data, based on the time that has elapsed, I believe?"

"Sure thing, Mr Wiggins. It'll take only a few moments," and she pulled out her pad, swiped the interface over onto the large screen in order to share the data and then joined the others, standing at the screen and working on the coordinates. "So, with the programming that I had put in place, that needs to have..." her voice tailed off as she thought, then her fingers flashed over the screen and a new set of coordinates and settings appeared. "Here we go..." and she dragged the settings across to Wiglet's panel area where he set things in motion.

"Now, I need someone to communicate with the team in Beijing. Not Thien Thi, I guess! Glitch, could you open up some channels please and tell them where we are with this? Also tell them that putting the settings back in place here is easier than unlocking their access - we have no idea how that has been frozen."

"Sure thing, Mr W.!" said Glitch and he stepped aside to use his communicator. At the same time, Wiglet and Melody checked over their settings and then stood back.

"OK, folks," said Wiglet. "This is the acid test. I shall run the simulator on the system once to check all is well and then action the update to the navigation in T-minus 300 seconds from the point we set it going. Everyone all right with that?"

There was much nodding of agreement and Wiglet initialised the test, watching every metric to make sure they'd not missed anything. "Here we go," and he set the test in motion. On the screen, the representation of the asteroid and its view of the Earth began to swing on a different trajectory. "Bear in mind that this is speeded up ten times, so we shall not see this effect so clearly."

The swing stopped and the asteroid was clearly pointing past the Earth so, Wiglet then announced, "Now we speed up even more so we can check that it will hitch a slingshot on the Earth's gravitational pull," and so saying, he adjusted the speed and the asteroid appeared to swing behind the Earth and then gather speed and shoot away into space.

"Finally, we check whether the trajectory is on track for the landing site on Mars. So let's crank up the speed ratio again," and as he said this, he increased the time factor to 5000 times. The asteroid hurtled through space and in due course, Mars flew into view, at which point, Wiglet slowed down the simulation and they all viewed the planet filling the screen as the huge rock plummeted toward the surface, right onto the impact zone that had been clearly defined in the original navigation. There was no impact of course and the simulation simply stopped.

"All's well with the data as far as I can see," said Wiglet. "Any comments, team? No? Then, we'll just..." but Wiglet was unable to finish his sentence as a massive, thundering noise smashed into the room and the airlock door in the lobby disintegrated into a pile of dust. Outside, standing and surveying the wreckage with piggy eyes, the Cryomorph geared itself up for the next blast.

Chapter Forty-two

"This way please," said Wiglet as he stood up calmly from where he had been sitting. "I rather anticipated that this might happen, so I have taken some precautions." The Cryomorph was building up to send another blast of powerful energy into the home and it moved back a few steps while it recharged. "It's safe for a few moments, my friends and, in that time, I can take you to safety."

"I'm not going out there while it's standing looking at me," said Glitch, anxiously.

"No need, Glitch. I have a plan," responded Wiglet as Xalata and Melody looked on with their mouths open in shock from the attack. Brett was holding onto Castrana, but Wiglet said, "Really, Brett I think Ms Machin can make her mind up what she wants to do now. It's certain that she can't do us any harm and she always has the option of the quick exit, if she fancies that." He nodded towards the wrecked door. "Now, let's be speedy, this way," and he led them to the bedroom furthest from the entry.

"Why are we going in here?" said Xalata, "This is just a bedroom and doesn't go anywhere at all."

"On the contrary, Xalata, it goes everywhere we want, look!" and he pointed to the corner of the room where a small panel was set near the floor. "Come in, come in. Shut the door. Now..." Wiglet pulled out a small control unit, touched a few elements on the surface and a moment later, the far wall of the room shimmered, brightened and then gave forth a dazzling light that had them all shielding their eyes.

"A portal? Here?" said Melody, "How does that work?"

"Quite simple, Melody. A portal can be anywhere to anywhere, if you have the technology, but it is incredibly dangerous unless you are absolutely certain what you are doing. Our friend Fark has found that his portal has disappeared. The simple reason is that it's here. Each portal is programmed with its own identity and termini. This one happens to now be owned by me since I deregistered it from its original owner, which was the Lunar Corporation. That's where Fark stole it from, for his own purposes."

"So Fark can't control it any more?" asked Brett, "And we can use it to travel?"

"Yes, and we had best do it swiftly, because I can hear that thing preparing to blast again," and sure enough, a rumbling outside told its own story as the Cryomorph stood itself once more in front of the home entrance and focussed on its target.

Wiglet stepped through the now open portal and arrived in an atrium not dissimilar to the one that was adjacent to the home they were leaving. The others hurried after him and, when they were all through, Wiglet closed the portal, just as they all heard another terrific blast.

"So, where are we?" said Xalata, looking around, and then she gasped, "Oh, I know!" That's the entry to the Control Room!" and she dashed across the atrium and flung open the airlock door into the entry. The others followed behind, looking a little dazed and displaced after having been 'jumped' to another location.

Brett was still hanging onto Castrana who was evidently getting very irritated by being hauled around the place. "Let me go, you oaf!" she spat as he dragged her to the Control Room.

"Absolutely not. I want you to see this little game played out to the end. Your great master, the Lord Asttar will mebbe need to pull his socks up if he's going to stop us unbelievers foiling his plans, don't you think?"

They walked into the Control Room and Wiglet and Glitch were already surveying the big screen and unlocking the access from there. "OK," said Glitch, we'll try again. We have 300 seconds once we start the programme and then the asteroid will begin to track away from the Earth. Simulator was OK - yes?"

"Indeed," said Wiglet "and I think we should activate as soon as possible, for I fear that the other protagonist in this little drama will not be long in arriving."

"Oh, so true," came the by now familiar voice of Fark, sneering as he spoke. "Stand aside, children and let the grownups take over the controls."

Glitch reached to press the activation element on the screen, but Castrana suddenly dived away from Brett, ripping her sleeve as she dragged her arm out of his grip. "Oh no you don't!" and she threw herself at Glitch, knocking him to the floor. Brett sprang forward but Fark stepped between him and Castrana, holding the EDW in front of him in a threatening way. "You really don't want to find out how this feels, Brett. Now, stand back against the unit over there - all of you! Castrana, relieve them of the keys and anything else that might be useful to them."

Melody and Xalata looked at each other, their brains racing. The programme just needed to be activated and the threat of destruction of the Earth would be gone. But they were trapped and Castrana was taking advantage of the fact that everyone was under Fark's control to push everyone into place by the unit. "Come on, little daughter," she crooned at Xalata. "Mummy's taking you for a walk."

"You're not my mother," hissed Xalata, "even if the biology says you are. I wouldn't have a warped parasite like you for a parent even if..."

Castrana slapped her suddenly and hard, leaving a red mark on her face and bringing unwilling tears to Xalata's eyes. "Quieten down, creature. You need to learn respect for your elders."

Brett glared at her and said, "I regret the day I ever set eyes on you, Castrana. You've been evil since the day we got together and I was too blinded to see it. The only thing I don't regret is Xally. I'm proud to say she's my daughter."

"Idiot!" muttered Castrana and she focused her gaze back on Xalata. "As for you, watch your step. I don't tolerate backchat from little girls." Xalata forced herself to keep her gaze and to look defiant, even though inside she was breaking up. She didn't dare speak in case her voice sounded broken, but she continued to hold Castrana's attention unblinkingly. Castrana broke her gaze away, unable to stand Xalata's frank, appraising look. "Empty your pockets, all of you! Stick it all on here," and she indicated a work surface at the other side of the room. Everyone did as they were bid.

Melody, meanwhile, was horrified by the treatment of her friend and was looking for any way that she could break free, activate the programme and enable her friends to escape. No ideas came and she sank into a depressed and defeated sulk, which, she knew, would not do any good, but just summed up the way, she felt.

Fark spoke again, waving the EDW in their general direction. "Now I 'ave your full attention, let's get some data, shall we? Since you 'ave been meddling, things 'ave moved on considerably. The asteroid is now well on its way and we 'ave only to wait another couple of hours before it's past the point of no return and will be dragged into the Earth by gravitational pull. Therefore, ladies and gentlemen, boys and girls, we're going to sit and wait. Now, sit on the floor!" and he pointed to the floor in front of the unit.

"Melody!" whispered Xalata, "what are we going to do?" There was no reply from her friend whose face was long and her eyes were full of tears. "Melody!"

"Be quiet!" said Fark. "No talking. I trust you not one little bit. You, Xala-taar. Move over here."

"Xal-atta," she muttered as she shifted over, separate from Melody.

*   *   *   *   *

The asteroid slid silently on, subtle corrections being made constantly by its on-board fusion engines tied in with its programmed navigation system. Because it was not of an even shape, the rotation of the rock could deflect it from its target by small degrees, but now, with intelligent navigation on board, it was homing in on its target and heading for the point of no return.

In front of it, the orb of the Earth grew larger by the moment, starting to be a major feature of its viewpoint. Within the next few hours it would be caught, inescapably, in the gravitational pull of the blue planet and, in that embrace, the Earth was sealing its own destruction.

On it sped, implacable, unstoppable and yet quite visible from an expectant Earth which saw its coming and trembled.

*   *   *   *   *

Wiglet raised his eyebrows. He was being signalled by Brett and was not really getting the message. Brett was desperately trying to get Wiglet to make some sort of diversion, attract Fark's attention, but Wiglet was just not understanding the frantic waggling of facial features that was going on. Risking being seen, Brett pointed at Fark and then at Wiglet and indicated that he should go to him.

After a moment of puzzlement, Wiglet finally got it and stood up from where he had been seated and walked across the room towards Fark. "Erm, Mr Fark..."

"I told you to sit down and stay put, now, do it!" and Fark waved the EWD in a threatening manner.

"I'm so sorry," continued Wiglet, "But there's a matter of needing to use the local facilities for some of us. Particularly those of us who are older."

Fark looked at Wiglet quizzically and then waved over Castrana. "He needs the loo. Take 'im and watch 'im."

"I'm not going on pee duty!" exclaimed Castrana. "Do it yourself," and she walked back to where she had been watching the large screen.

"It's not as if I have anywhere to run away to, now is it?" asked Wiglet. "I just need to go to the facilities over there and then return and sit down."

"I'll follow you to the door," said Fark, "No tricks or one of these little girlies is going to get hurt!"

"No tricks, of course," replied Wiglet as he began to walk towards the entrance that led to the toilets, passing Brett as he did so. Fark followed at a distance, holding the EWD in front of him and, just as he passed Brett he was hit from behind by Brett's weight flying at him in an attempt to overbalance him. Fark stumbled, fell, twisted around swiftly and pointed the EWD straight at Brett and pulled the trigger. A buzz, a flash and a smell of electrical discharge filled the room and Brett fell to the floor with a groan.

Xalata leapt to her feet and ran to her father with a cry, but Fark was already on his feet and pointing the weapon at Xalata. "If you know what's good for you, *my dear*, you'll sit right back down and shut up! And you, Wiggins, you deserve a dose of this too. Sit down and 'old it." Xalata had no choice; she looked at her Dad who was evidently in pain, but still conscious and trying to sit up. Wiglet put his arm around her and started to walk her back to where they had been seated.

"You wait, Fark. Just you wait..."

"Mm, thank you my dear. I am of course utterly terrified by the threats of a schoolgirl."

Meanwhile, Melody had sat quiet all the time and was staring at the floor, underneath a unit, not far from where Fark had fallen. Xalata came and sat next to her and Glitch, muttering. While Fark continued to threaten Brett and Castrana watched the screen, Melody whispered, "Under there, look," and she pointed with her eyes.

"What? Can't see anything," whispered Xalata.

"Something fell out of his pocket when your Dad knocked him over. It's slid under there."

Xalata peered and, eventually, could make out the shape of something under the unit, within reach, but needing one of them to move over there. In a flash she had an idea and...

"You maggot! I'm not your friend any more!" she yelled at Melody who looked at her with wide eyes full of shock and surprise. "I can't believe you said that. You make me sick!" And she jumped to her feet and strode over to where the unit stood.

Melody, suddenly realising what Xalata was doing, responded in kind, "Well rid of you, you stuck up little insect. Go see what your Daddy wants," and she leered at Xalata across the room.

The rest of the group in the room stared with mouths open as if they had been struck. "OK, ok. Calm down girlies, let's 'ave a bit of peace and quiet 'ere," said Fark and he turned back to Brett.

Xalata wasted not a moment and, sitting with her back to the unit, reached around and groped for the object that Fark had lost. At first, she could feel nothing and then reached behind with her other hand, all the time keeping her eye on Fark and Castrana. Glitch and Melody meanwhile, looked on anxiously while Wiglet, who had no idea what was going on, simply sat with a puzzled look on his face. "I really do need to go, actually," he muttered.

Then with a triumphant beam on her face, Xalata pulled out what her hand had discovered under the unit - it was some sort of control unit and, at first, she had no idea what it was. Fearful that the two captors would spot her, she kept glancing at it and then back at them, trying to work out what it was. Moments later, her face beamed with delight as she realised - it was the control for the Cryomorph.

She looked up at Melody, glanced across at Fark and then, looking back at Melody, squinted her eyes and made explosive puffing expressions with her face. Melody, of course had no idea what she was trying to convey and looked at her friend in puzzlement. "What?" she mouthed, screwing her face up in lack of understanding.

Xalata tried to mime walking heavily while sitting down - not the easiest feat - and then, looking across at Fark, waved her arms in a mime of an explosion, her mouth and eyes indicating the bang. Melody suddenly got it and her eyes lit with excitement. She pointed at the control and then at Xalata and then at the floor, indicating *bring it here*.

Fark suddenly turned and saw the two looking at each other, "'Ere, you two. I thought you weren't friends. Stop the comms right now and sit quiet. You, Wiggins, on your feet. I don't want a mess on the floor so I'm taking you to the loo right now - if anyone else needs to go, join the queue. Any tricks and one of you gets really hurt. Orbit here was lucky that I had the zapper on low power otherwise he'd 'ave been in real trouble."

Melody immediately stood up. "Er, I'd like to go too, please, Mr Fark," and she walked over to join Wiglet as they were ushered to the toilets by Fark.

Xalata seized her chance and studied the control carefully, out of sight of Castrana. It was simple. The screen showed the viewpoint from the Cryomorph, which appeared to be ambling aimlessly around the atriums of the habitat. The main features of the dashboard were three elements: location coordinates for the Cryomorph which showed it was still in the region of the home where they had been held; an entry point for new coordinates and a pulldown for actions to be associated with the arrival of the Cryomorph at the destination. She quickly entered the location of the Control Centre, selected *Destroy* and then from a visual map, selected the exact location of the door. The *Confirm* command sent the instructions and a message came back to say they had been received, just as the others came back from the loos. On the screen, she could see that the beast had already sprung into action and was on the move.

She tucked the control into her pocket and then stood to welcome back the others. "Sorry, Melody. It's just the stress of being held here by these *criminals*," and she hugged her friend, whispering, "It's on its way!"

Chapter Forty-three

"There are forty minutes left until the asteroid will be gripped by Earth's gravity," reported Glitch.

"Thanks for the update, brat, but we know where it is and what it's doing. We're in control now and not you any more," leered Fark.

"Yes, be quiet," echoed Castrana, rather pointlessly. It seemed that she felt out of the limelight at the moment and wanted to make an impact on the group, but Fark was definitely in control and the EWD ensured that he stayed that way. No one fancied risking a blast of high voltage electricity for his or her pains.

Melody and Xalata however were quiet, expectantly waiting a change of fortunes for their little group. Fark was not paying them any attention so they had time to think what they would do when the game changed. They'd not alerted Brett, Wiglet or Glitch who were unaware of what would happen in a very short time. The reason for this was simple: Fark had made them sit apart from the two girls and therefore they couldn't communicate. Nor did they want to risk another pantomime where they tried to communicate what was happening, so they decided that silence was the best solution at this point.

 Xalata didn't dare look at the control she had tucked away in a sealed pocket of her suit. She knew roughly how far away the beast had been, but had no clue as to how long it would take to arrive.

Fark and Castrana were watching the display intently, seeing the orb of the Earth grow bigger in the view from the asteroid. There was silence in the room as each of them contemplated the fate that awaited Earth. Glitch looked defeated and Brett looked very angry yet powerless - the electric jolt from the EWD had sapped his strength and he was now in no position to tackle their two captors. Meanwhile, Wiglet was lost in his own thoughts although his gaze kept flashing across to the surface where their possessions, emptied from their pockets, had been dumped.

The minutes ticked by and Glitch became ever more anxious. "Thirty minutes," he whispered to Wiglet who grimaced in response. There seemed to be no way to stop the evil deed that was about to be committed.

Down on Earth, undoubtedly, they would be trying to marshal together the resources to destroy the asteroid before it hit the planet. However, the four hours that they would have left after Earth's gravitational pull had seized hold of the giant rock would be too little to make any effective response before impact destroyed Beijing and laid waste to huge areas of the continent.

Xalata fidgeted and made to stand up, but Melody grabbed her and whispered, "Stay put. We don't want to distract their attention from the screen. The shock needs to be at maximum."

She sat back down again and waited. She was not a patient girl at the best of times and she was just wondering what their next step would be after the impact when there was the most enormous explosion, deafening everyone in the room and sending debris flying about, crashing into walls, breaking equipment and falling onto the team as they huddled with fear.

A part of a door flew across the room and hit Fark squarely on the head, felling him at a stroke. Castrana was lacerated by flying glass and shrieked in horror as blood streamed from her face and hands.

The moment the captives realised what had happened, they leapt into action, led by the two girls who had been ready for the shock. "Quick!" yelled Xalata, "we must get back to the cell that we were in, assuming that the Cryomorph hasn't destroyed that too."

The shocked adults stumbled to their feet, but no one was injured seriously. Sitting on the floor had protected them from the blast and now their main objective was to get out of that place and back to the home where they had set up base previously.

Wiglet came to his senses and set about opening the portal once more, which suddenly and magically appeared in one of the damaged walls. Xalata pulled out the Cryomorph control and said, "Let's finish the job," and entered some simple commands into the interface. Then all of them dived through the portal, just as another explosion rocked the Control Room and destroyed what was left of the equipment in there.

*   *   *   *   *

With only minutes to spare, they arrived back in the room they had left only an hour or so before, to find it badly messed up, but still largely intact. Glitch ran across to the big screen on the far wall and logged into the controls once more. Everything seemed to be operational.

"Now, young people," said Wiglet, with a serious expression, "we have one chance at this. My understanding is that the programming we have put in place for the course change will update on current position parameters. Therefore we should have no need to recalculate. Am I correct?"

There were some nervous nods around the room.

"Melody, Xalata? Can you confirm that is the case please?"

Melody responded nervously, "Yes, Mr Wiggins, I believe it is the case." She glanced at Xalata who nodded firmly. They both knew the importance of what they were doing and didn't want to foul up at this point.

"Very well," continued Wiglet, "in that case we shall activate the programme that we have already tested. Glitch, if you please..." and he indicated to Glitch that he should prepare the sequence for activation. With a few swipes on the screen, all elements were in place and the *Activate* button glowed red under Glitch's hand.

"Ready to go, Mr Wiggins."

"Very well, let's do it!"

Glitch touched the screen and the button faded to show a progress vector that indicated how the course would change in the coming minutes and hours. "Let's call up the on board cameras," he said and, so saying, brought up the screen that gave the view of the ever-swelling Earth.

"Nothing seems to be happening," said Melody, anxiously.

"That's because the signals need to arrive there, then be processed. Then the effects of the engines firing will only take place very gradually," responded Glitch. "Let's check the engine view." Sure enough, the engines could be seen, leaving a trail of plasma from the increased thrust that was pushing the rock away from its former trajectory and on to a new path. "We'll see the change in about half an hour, I would guess. Let's focus on the left edge of the Earth's disk and put a marker on the screen that shows its relative position, then we can see what's happening. How do I drop a marker on there?" he asked no one in particular.

Searching through the on screen toolkit, he could not find anything that would do the task. Wiglet scratched his head and Melody furrowed her brow as they tried to address this simple, but infuriatingly baffling puzzle. Suddenly, Xalata jumped to her feet, picked a pen off the table and walked over to the screen. "Low tech is sometimes better," she said as she drew a line exactly on the edge of the Earth's left-hand horizon.

"Indeed it is," agreed Wiglet and they all laughed. "Now, we just need to wait."

*   *   *   *   *

"So what happened to Fark and his evil henchwoman?" asked Xalata as they sat and waited.

"Who cares?" said Glitch, "They're out of our hair and I for one would like never to see the two of them again."

"Yeah, that's all very well, but we're better than them, aren't we?"

"Well, yeah, duh!"

"So, shouldn't we be concerned that they may be injured or worse...?"

Glitch shrugged, "I dunno, we've got enough on our plates here without watching out for the bad guys too."

"You're quite right," said Brett, joining in the conversation from across the room. "We should find out what's happened to them, now that we are fairly certain we have succeeded in foiling their plan."

"Indeed, we have succeeded," said Wiglet, "because I can now see that the Earth's disk has moved to the right away from Xalata's mark on the screen. We are on track! Now we just need to ensure nothing happens to stop that process. I've informed Mission Control down in Beijing and I think we have managed to hand over control to them now - we're just waiting for confirmation of that. Then our work here is done and we can discover how best to get back home."

"Surely, we'll just jump using the portal?" said Melody.

"Definitely not, Melody. I think it would be unwise for us to challenge the portal this much at this point. Each jump is literally a gamble, particularly with so many of us. I am not convinced that we would be safe in making such a significant jump back home."

"So how are we going to get back then?" said Xalata. "We can't take a TransTrak because it's not out here any more since the habitat was closed off."

"There may be another way," said Wiglet, mysteriously. "Meanwhile, I think we should send out a mission to check on the Control Room - what's left of it."

Between them, they worked out that Brett was probably strong enough now to tackle the trip back to the Control Room and he would take the two girls with him while Glitch and Wiglet looked after the asteroid. The three of them trooped out of the home and picked up the truck that stood outside and, with Melody in control, swept off to see what had happened to their foes.

*   *   *   *   *

As they stepped off the truck at the shattered Control Room entrance, a deep sense of foreboding fell over them. Xalata now felt awful that she had sent the Cryomorph to continue its destruction, knowing that Fark and her mother were still inside. What had become of them? She soon found out.

The devastation of the entry and the area immediately inside was massive - great blocks of material had been dashed from the walls, melted metal was spattered on the floor and a smell of burning plastics hung in the air, leaving an unpleasant choking feeling in their throats. They covered their mouths and noses with their hands and walked forward. The lighting had been damaged and Melody pulled out a tiny torch that lit the way down the exploded corridor, over rubble and into the now devastated Control Room.

It was barely recognisable - the huge screen at the far end had melted into streaks that layered the wall in fanciful colours, like some abstract artist's unhinged work; the large units, behind which they had hidden, had also been shattered and there was no sign of any of the smaller items of equipment which appeared to have been vaporised in the blast.

Xalata looked around anxiously, hoping against hope that the two villains had made good their escape. There appeared to be no sign, but, as they split up to search the wreckage, there came a shout from Brett, "Over here!" As they dashed over, Xalata could see an arm pushed out from underneath some rubble, clad in a torn Scramsuit - black, with silver markings. It was her mother's, Castrana's.

She gasped and a torrent of mixed emotions hit her, "I ... oh no ... she's," and she bent down to feel the bloodied hand that was the only sign of the body lying trapped beneath. "It's cold," she said flatly, knowing the implication of what she had discovered. "I've killed her."

Brett stood up and gathered her to him in a big hug, trying to comfort her, but the tears were pouring down her face and she pushed away, desperately trying to keep control of her emotions.

Melody moved towards her, "Xalata, you couldn't have known..."

"Don't be stupid! Of course I knew. I just touched the command and that beast killed them. *I* killed them. No one else."

"They were going to destroy the world, Xalata," Melody continued. "If you plan crimes as big as that, then the ending's never going to be good, whichever way it goes. You helped stop them..."

"Yes, by killing them," sobbed Xalata, "Is that the right way? Is it?" She turned away, unable to speak any more while Brett tried to move some of the rubble that had buried Castrana.

"We've not found Fark," he observed, "although he may be in here somewhere, under the broken walls and equipment."

Xalata turned and looked at Brett, "I don't feel bad about him. He was an evil worm and if he's had his come-uppance, so be it. But, I've killed my mother and, even though she was an evil witch who didn't care about me, how do you think that makes me feel? How does it make *you* feel?"

There was no answer that Brett could easily give, no comforting words, so he chose to remain silent and now, with relief, Xalata came to him and allowed herself to be comforted. They stood, a silent tableau: Xalata and Brett, with Melody watching quietly as her friend dealt with the turmoil in her head.

*   *   *   *   *

Fark crawled. He couldn't walk. When the beast had attacked the Control Room he was struck dumb with horror at the thought that the Cryomorph was out of control. He had searched his pockets for the control unit, but it wasn't there and he had quickly realised that it must have fallen out during the attack by Brett. But who had grabbed it and then turned the beast on its own master?

He was too tired and in too much pain to care at this point as he crawled. He had pulled himself away from the Control Room and further down the corridor that led away from the damaged airlock entry. He had no clue what was down there, but he knew that he had to be out of the way or risk being discovered. He looked back and saw that, although he was leaving a few small spots, there was little blood showing where he had dragged himself. The dust that was in the air was settling rapidly so his tracks were being covered as he moved away.

What could he do now? The controls for the asteroid were set, but he wasn't certain that Wiglet and the interfering kids couldn't break into the code to stop the asteroid's progress toward the Earth. He had no way to communicate, no way to know whether his mission had been successful. He was injured, without equipment and without a means of escape.

He had no idea what he could do. But he was about to find out.

*　　　*　　　*　　　*　　　*

"So, what happened, Dad?" asked Xalata, as she pushed away gently from him. "How did it all go wrong ... with Castrana, I mean?"

"Hmm. Long story, Xally. I'm not sure you're ready for it yet."

"I just killed her, Dad. I think I'm probably ready for most anything at this point, don't you?"

"Yes, I see what you mean. Well, your mother was stunningly beautiful when she was in her early twenties ... and knew it. She could be with any man she wanted and she seemed to be with a lot, over the time I knew her before we got together. Why she got her hooks into me, I'm not sure. She seemed to be lured by the fact that I worked at the LunarBase, although at that time I was on furlough on Earth."

"Where were you living then?"

"In the United Kingdom, in a little village about 10K away from my work. She suddenly appeared in the village and had her sights set on me. What was I supposed to do? She was more beautiful than any other woman who had ever showed any interest in me. We began dating and the inevitable happened. Then she declared that she was pregnant - I was horrified. I'd no way of supporting her, I lived a fairly chaotic life, between Earth and the Moon and I couldn't see how it would work.

"Anyway, we got married and you were born not long after. At that point, everything seemed to change. She had always been very interested in talking to me about my work, which struck me as odd because what I do is completely different from her field of expertise - she's brilliant ... was brilliant - and so I had the impression that she was always pumping me for information. We would have awful rows about it ... and about everything else. We were not even a little bit compatible and she made it clear that she hated being with me.

"Basically, we split up; you went to your Aunt's who was delighted to look after you and I returned to the work I was doing. But it didn't stop there. She and Fark tried to blackmail me into diverting lithium products to their camp on Farside so they could, now I realise, continue to build their monsters like the Cryomorph."

"Why the lithium?" asked Xalata.

"It's a very valuable element that is used in a whole raft of things here on the Moon, not least of all in purifying the air, but also in nuclear fusion and in the production of a much rarer element, Tritium. The fusion reactors are essential to deliver all the power that these two, along with their accomplices, needed to go on with their evil projects."

"So did they get the lithium?"

"They had been progressively stealing it over a couple of years. Because Fark was in charge of security, he could arrange to divert supplies and cook the records so that no one would know. But then it became evident that there were quantities of the stuff going missing and everything had to be clamped down. That's when they came up with the plan to get me to provide it through my legitimate channels. Naturally, I said no and that's when the whole thing kicked off, they kidnapped you and at the same time, were undertaking their insane plan to destroy the Earth."

"Quite how they would have survived without the Earth to support them, I don't understand?"

"They didn't care. They believed that the Lord Asttar would look after them and all would be well. He would provide a place on Earth that was free from the devastation. Utter nonsense, but they believed it."

Xalata nodded her head, smiled at her father and then went across to where Melody was sitting, waiting. "Sorry, my friend, but I'm a bit fried by all of this."

"Not surprising really."

"No, I s'pose not, but you've been amazing. What's with the 'scared of her own shadow' act and then coming on like a superhero?"

"I don't like my friends and family being threatened and I guess that in those circumstances you forget about being afraid and you just do it. Come on, you're the same."

"Nope - I'm not. I just have a big mouth and don't engage my brain before I speak ... or act. You're the real hero here, Melody. Thanks, um, y'know, for being a good mate."

Melody smiled and gave her friend a hug. This was going to be a lifetime friendship.

*   *   *   *   *

Fark struggled and sat up, the pain in his legs getting worse, where he had been hit by a piece of flying debris as the Cryomorph destroyed the Control Room. He managed to rest himself against the blank surface of a corridor wall and reviewed his options. He was immobilised, had no communications because he'd lost all his devices in the explosions, was injured and had no clear way of getting back to the LunarBase. And even if he did manage to get back there, he would probably be arrested on sight as the do-gooder, Brett Orbit, would have blabbed his name to the authorities.

He felt grim. His mood was low, his legs pained him and he had no options. What was he to do? As he sat there, feeling sorry for himself, he noticed a dim light coming from further down the corridor - possibly a room or an entry into another atrium. As he had never explored this end of the area, he was reluctant to expend the energy and suffer the pain of moving in that direction, but what else was there to do?

So, pulling himself over onto his stomach again, he continued to drag his body along the corridor by the strength in his arms and by pushing with one foot that could still take some pressure. As he got nearer to the light, he could see that it was an atrium and, on rounding the corner of the entry, he saw something that made his heart leap.

It was a plain double door - operated electronically, but able to take a reasonably large number of people through the entry. This sort of door was only ever used in one place throughout Luna - the TransTrak! He knew that the TransTrak didn't run any more, but it was a route away from where he sat currently, so he pulled himself across to the doors, operated their lock mechanism and, to his surprise, found that the doors slid back to reveal a staircase down to the TransTrak 'tube' which was sited below all the other structures on the LunarBase.

The steps were a challenge, but he discovered that his best way of tackling them was to sit down and bump down on his bottom. They didn't descend very far before he came out into the single line station of the deserted track. There was dim emergency lighting but that afforded enough light for him to see that the tunnel was still all intact.

It was spooky down in that dimly-lit sub-lunar burrow, every sound he made echoing down the tube in front of and behind him, every flicker of light imagined or real dancing up like ghosts in front of his eyes. The optical tricks grew to such an extent that he had to close his eyes momentarily in order to steady his senses. It was then that he noticed another door, set back into the curved wall of the tunnel and on the other side of the track from him. In all his journeys on the TransTrak, he'd never seen a door set into the tunnel before and he was intrigued.

He cursed his injured legs and shuffled over to the trackside so that he could see the door more clearly. It was curved, like the wall and it bore a symbol, which he recognised as the universal sign for 'Keep Out'. He couldn't see how the door opened, but he was determined to find out so, shuffling his legs over onto the track, he lowered himself down and then crawled across the guide rails before ending up in front of the door. No one was likely to have ever opened this portal while Habitat 14 was running and populated, because it was forbidden to step onto the TransTrak tracks.

Now he had the opportunity and he pushed himself against the door to see whether it would move inwards. To his great surprise, it did and he fell forward and tumbled down a set of around ten steps, landing winded, angry and in pain, even more. Looking around him, an idea came to him and his face brightened. "I know where I am!" he exclaimed, although there was no one to hear.

Chapter Forty-four

"What do we do next and how do we get back to LunarBase?" Xalata was starting to come back to her normal self a little, although every time she had seen that hand sticking from the rubble, her face had darkened and her mood had dropped. But now they were back at the home, with Wiglet and Glitch. They had told them the whole terrible tale and the mood had been sombre for a while, but had lifted when it was clear that the asteroid was now heading around the Earth and would slingshot using the Earth's gravity to send it on its path to Mars. "We are on Farside, for Frank's sake. How do we head back to Nearside?"

"Not with the portal, I'm afraid," said Wiglet. "I risked it twice because we were in danger, but tempting fate with a third jump, particularly that far, would be unwise. However, I have an idea, as I mentioned earlier." Everyone paid rapt attention and gathered round him as he spoke.

"I had mentioned that the TransTrak ran while this habitat was in operation. When it was abandoned - this happened for a number of reasons, but mostly because certain parts of it had become unusable because of faults in the construction - the TransTrak of course was stopped. It had never run between LunarBase and here in any case as this had been a separately supplied base which received its own missions from Earth to provision it."

"So, this base was completely separate from everything that LunarBase did?" asked Glitch.

"Yes, indeed. It was totally self-sufficient which was partly its benefit but also in that lay the seeds of its destruction. Cut off, it was not so well run and maintained and consequently the problems that started small, grew into ones that affected the quality of life. Now, you might ask, why then does it seem perfectly fine for us here?"

"Beat me to it," said Xalata.

"The simple answer is that there are so few of us here that we make very little impact on the ecosystem. Our needs are tiny compared to a full population of researchers, scientists and support staff. That runs into hundreds of people per habitat."

"So, this doesn't tell us anything about how you'll get us out of here...?" said Melody.

"No, but it's not just my responsibility, I think," answered Wiglet. "I was talking about the TransTrak - it's no longer running, but there was another tunnel, cut accidentally many years ago, by an out of control suite of nanobots that had been programmed to build a route and then stop. They continued cutting the tunnel, unstoppably until it circumnavigated the whole Moon. That tunnel, I know, passes below this habitat. And, more importantly, it passes below LunarBase on Nearside."

"Then we can catch the train home," shouted Xalata, excitedly.

"Not quite, Xalata. There never were any trains - it was never commissioned. There was a huge fuss of course because of the unnecessary work that had been done, but when all's said and done, nanobots that are using the environment they work in for building materials don't actually consume anything - so there was no real cost. The original plan was abandoned for a number of reasons, but there had never been a need to commission a full service on that tunnel."

"So let me get this straight," said Brett. "There's a tunnel below us that goes right around the Moon and passes beneath our home base? But it doesn't have any vehicles on it?"

"Correct, but I have a solution for that too."

"Let me guess. Let me guess!" shouted Xalata, getting very excited now, probably as a reaction to her former state of mind. "We get a truck down there and we ride home."

"In theory, yes, but you have to remember that the distance from here to LunarBase is around 6000 kilometres."

"No truck is going to manage that and anyway, how long would that take? What's the truck's top speed?" asked Melody.

"About 60kph," answered Wiglet.

"Ouch - 100 hours of driving. Over four days continuous. No stations, no food or water."

"Exactly, so that plan is not really feasible, unless we provision up and are willing to endure a good deal of discomfort and distress. So, I have a further thought." The group listened eagerly. "I know that the TransTrak engineers have used the redundant tunnel as a test bed for new vehicles and..."

"We contact the engineers and get them to send us a train!" squealed Xalata, very uncharacteristically. "Help, I must calm down. Sorry guys, I'm a bit wound up."

"Correct on both counts," smiled Wiglet. "So, what are we waiting for? Glitch, the comms panel please." And Wiglet proceeded to patch them through to the TransTrak engineers and, within ten minutes, had made clear to them their situation and had ordered up a train. "Around 4 hours before they can get everything up and working, then the prototype train will travel around the track at a slower than normal speed of about 600kph and then we shall be in business! All we have to do is to find the entry point."

"14 hours then," said Xalata, a little more calmly. They all settled down to wait.

*	*	*	*	*

Fark's excitement had been tempered with a dose of reality. Yes, he had found the abandoned circular tunnel, but ... he had no means of transport and he was unlikely to be able to get a truck down there to drive back, even knowing that it would take forever to get home. "Still, no getting lost, whichever way I go," he chuckled to himself and then listened to the echoes reverberate down the narrow tunnel.

He realised that he was in a bad position and decided that, before he either climbed out of there or struck out along the tunnels in the hope of finding a solution, he would sit down and think.

He was free, for the moment, and he intended to stay that way. He'd had enough of the smartarse kids, the self-righteous Orbit and the frankly idiotic Wiggins. So, steering clear of them would be good. He did still have his two henchmen who performed menial tasks and did the heavy lifting, but they were a good way from there and he didn't fancy trying to find them when he had such reduced mobility.

So, sitting and thinking was probably the best plan.

*	*	*	*	*

Later that day, after they had rested and had some food, they set about planning their exit. Finding the entry to the TransTrak had been simple. Glitch had summoned up the plans on the screen and they had virtual-walked the route that was indicated, arriving in the abandoned TransTrak station and then identifying the hidden door on the other side of the track.

"Easy-peasy," said Melody. "Let's go."

"I think you're forgetting something Melody," said Brett. "We shall need to report the death of Castrana and then the authorities can come and recover her body. So, I suggest we take some video of the area and the devastation. In addition, the Cryomorph cannot be left to wander this area alone..."

"Erm, I have a plan for that too," said Wiglet with his mysterious look again. "Where will the Cryomorph go?"

"Well, anywhere we want it to - I still have the control," said Xalata.

"And where is it now?"

"Wandering the corridors around the area of the Control Room. I can pinpoint it exactly if you want."

"No need, Xalata, however, I shall need you to bring it to a place that I shall specify in due course."

"OK," she responded slowly, "and then what?"

"We shall deal with it."

They were all intrigued but it was evident that Wiglet wanted to keep his cards close to his chest, so they humoured him and pretended to not be too interested.

"I shall need to go and prepare for a little while, then I shall give you instructions, if that is OK?"

"Sure thing," said Xalata, "whatever you say, Mr Wiggins."

*   *   *   *   *

Wiglet's plan was dangerous and he knew it. The Cryomorph was a creature made in the furnaces of Hell, or so it seemed to those who encountered it. So finding a way to trap it and destroy it would need devilish cunning and a good helping of very good luck. Wiglet was not the sort of person who left things to luck though. He'd been brought up with an analytical mind by scientific parents who gave him a top education, which had in turn sharpened that mind to make it a formidable weapon and tool.

His outward appearance was strange - wild-haired, small spectacles that were an anachronism in these days of laser-optimised sight - he was the epitome of a mad professor, but his looks belied his true nature. Now, he had set that mind to work and it was coming up with the goods. His prime objective was to keep everyone else safe - he, in his mind, was dispensable.

He left the home where the band of friends were still working on tidying up things before they moved on with the final chapter of their great adventure. As he left, he cast a glance back and smiled - *the future is safe in the hands of the upcoming generation*, he thought. Walking briskly away, he headed back to the atrium and then down one of the side corridors that led to a more deserted part of that section of the habitat. The lights were dim here because there was no passage of people to stimulate them into action.

Near the end of the corridor and through a large airlock, he found what he was looking for: a sizeable blank wall that faced the corridor and formed part of the outer structure of the habitat. This was just what he needed, knowing that the Cryomorph was virtually indestructible, even in the vacuum of space.

He bent down, near the bottom of the wall, and left a small flat panel in place, barely visible in the gloom. Then he checked the location, verified it with his pad and then called Melody.

"Melody, I am now ready for the Cryomorph. I would like you to take control of it please, if you would be so kind. I think that Xalata has probably had enough responsibility for a lifetime in controlling that beast."

"Sure thing, Mr Wiggins. Just let me get the controls and then you can give me the location." There was a pause as she spoke with Xalata, who gladly handed over the control. "OK, I'm ready - let me read you the current position of the creature." She checked the screen and saw that the Cryomorph was stationary, about 200 metres down a corridor away from the Control Room. "Yes, I've got its location - can you give me the coordinates where you want it please?"

Wiglet read out the exact location where he was standing and Melody read it back to him to check.

"Then I also need you to assign an action to it once it arrives."

"Oh, that's easy my dear. Just set it to *Destroy* If you would."

"Er, OK. You'll be well out of the way, won't you?" Melody sounded anxious.

"Naturally, I shall be in the area to see that all goes to plan."

"OK - if you are sure, I shall plug those commands in now and activate. Do you want a time schedule of when it'll arrive there?"

"Yes, that would be most useful."

"Activating now - it's on the move. The readout estimates 22 minutes for it to get to you."

"Perfect, thank you, Melody. Goodbye." And so saying, Wiglet cut the communication and prepared to wait for the beast.

*   *   *   *   *

Melody was unhappy. She had not liked Wiglet's 'Goodbye', nor the manner of his leaving. She turned to Xalata who had been following the dialogue. "What do you think?"

"I think he's up to something very dangerous..."

"D'you think we should follow him?"

"And do what? The Cryomorph will be with him in twenty minutes. What are we going to do?"

"Just make sure he's not putting himself in danger. Look, I have the coordinates, we can follow his route, but I'll keep an eye on the way the Cryomorph is going so we don't bump into each other." She glanced at the screen, "I ...oh no! It's going much faster than I thought. It's going to be with him in about five minutes. Quick! We need to hurry," and she dragged her friend to the door and hauled her out toward the atrium.

"Come on!" she yelled as Xalata gathered herself from the shock of being pulled through the doorway and she set off after the fast-disappearing figure of Melody. They ran together down the corridors, Melody checking every few moments to make sure that they were not on an intersecting path with the beast. "It's down this way, to the left," she cried as they turned into a smaller corridor. There were moments left before the beast was due to be with Wiglet.

They rounded a corner that led, through a large airlock, into a corridor beyond and there, facing away from them, stood the Cryomorph, its body shaking from the exertion of running to its programmed location and, in front of it, a sight that made the girls gasp with fear.

The end wall of the corridor seemed to be a blaze of light, edged with a shimmering border where two realities met. In the light beyond, the girls could see barely recognisable features - a large room, perhaps an atrium, with furniture and equipment, shimmering in the strange and eerie light.

"It's a portal," whispered Xalata, for fear of gaining the beast's attention. "But where's it go to?"

"Wiglet's tricking the Cryomorph into going through into another place, but where is it and won't it be just as dangerous there?" And then she stopped suddenly, for as their eyes became accustomed to the brightness of the portal's light, they could make out a wild-haired figure, standing on the other side, waving frantically. "What the freak's he doing?" shouted Melody, "it'll kill him!"

And sure enough, the beast seemed to be charging itself for a massive discharge to blast the tiny figure of Wiglet who, now, was jumping up and down, goading the beast and trying to lure it to him. The girls watched with their faces drained of colour as they realised what Wiglet was doing.

"He's going to get killed, luring it away," sobbed Melody, "we can't let him do it!"

"Don't be crazy! How do you think you are going to stop that huge creature now and ... look!" As Xalata spoke, the beast sat back on its haunches and then launched itself towards the portal. Its vast weight shook the ground and it hurled itself with a roar towards Wiglet, who now stood impassively, waiting for his doom.

As the beast crossed the boundary between that reality and the next, there was a huge flash of light that left the girls blinded momentarily and a rumbling roar as the wall collapsed where the portal had stood. The habitat was suddenly open to the vacuum of space and, with an abrupt hiss, the airlock door between the beast and the girls slammed shut, leaving only a small porthole to view the scene of devastation beyond. Dust filled the air and in moments, it was impossible to see anything in that space.

The girls sat on the floor and wept.

*   *   *   *   *

When they returned to the home to tell the story of Wiglet's brave end, the others were just closing up everything in preparation for the trek across to the TransTrak location that they had identified.

"But, why did he do that? We could have left the Cryomorph wandering here," said Glitch, "I don't get it."

"And we don't know where it's gone to either," said Brett.

"That's just it. Wherever the Cryomorph is, so is Wiglet. I just can't believe it," Melody sobbed.

"Come on, guys," said Xalata. We can't do any more. That place is blasted to hell and it's open to space in any case, so we can't go in. They're who knows where so we are wasting our time looking now. Let's head for the TransTrak and then we'll tell the people coming over what has happened and they can maybe solve the puzzle."

"Sound advice, Xally," said Brett. "We have everything from in here that we need. We know where we are going, so let's do it," and he set off to find the truck that would take them to the TransTrak.

Melody pulled herself together and the friends trotted after Brett, loaded the truck and headed for the station. It was not long before they found it, with its doors wide open. "Strange," said Brett, "I'd have thought this lot would be closed up since it was mothballed when everyone bailed out." He stepped off the truck and went to examine the doors. "It goes down to the platform. Come on!"

They all picked up their kit and hurried down the steps. It was eerie in the half-light, knowing that they were in a tunnel that had not been used for years. But Glitch had been doing his homework and he called, "This way!" and led them to the hidden entry to the redundant circular tunnel - again, the doors stood open, so it appeared not to be very hidden. Looking on the floor, Glitch stopped suddenly, "Just a mo'. What's this?" and he looked down at a couple of faint spots of red that shone on the floor in front of him.

"Looks like blood," said Brett. "You don't think..." but before he could say any more they all heard a shuffle and a groan from in the next tunnel.

"I *do* think," cried Xalata and she darted into the tunnel before anyone could stop her. There on the floor, between the tracks, lay Fark, sneering but obviously in pain.

"Well Zala-taar. Have you come to rescue me?"

"No, Fark. I'd sooner see you dead, but there's been quite enough of that for one day. Guys! Help me with him," and she jumped down to the tracks and grabbed Fark under his arms.

The others hurried along and, as they did so, they could hear a distant sound coming down the tunnel. "It's the TransTrak!" cried Melody.

"Leave him there," said Glitch with an evil scowl.

Fark suddenly screamed, "No! Help me, please!"

"And what help would you have been to the people on Earth, billions of them who would have died if you and your Asttarian nutters had had their way," said Xalata, dropping him again.

"No, I ... it's what we believe. We thought we were doing our Lord's bidding."

"Realising the error of your ways, huh, Fark?" said Xalata coldly. The sound grew louder as the TransTrak approached.

"Yes. Yes. Yes! Please help me out of here." His eyes were pleading and suddenly, the friends saw in his eyes the Fark that used to be, before he was corrupted by a strange and deviant ideology.

"Two wrongs don't make a right," declared Melody and hopped down onto the track. She and Xalata grabbed Fark and heaved him onto the platform and then leapt up there themselves, moments before the train pulled quietly into the station.

"Quite right," came a familiar voice as they all stood up again.

"Wiglet!" yelled Xalata and dashed over to the very dusty tutor and gave him a huge hug. "I mean, Mr Wiggins! What the ... what happened, where did you go, where's the Cryomorph..."

"Steady," said Wiglet, separating himself from the enthusiastic grasp of his pupil. "Let's just greet our newly arrived friends from Nearside, then I shall tell you the whole story on the journey back."

Chapter Forty-five

The TransTrak glided silently along, travelling onward in the same direction it had arrived in. The crew had decided that as they had traversed one half of the circumnavigation of the Moon, they might as well do the other half too.

The friends had all seated themselves in a carriage, with Fark secured to a rail, but sitting relatively comfortably, while Wiglet described what had happened.

"I knew that the only solution was to destroy the beast, otherwise it would either pursue us down these tunnels and then wreak havoc Nearside, or it would be a problem that someone else would have to deal with when they opened up Habitat 14 once again.

"I decided therefore that I would use the portal technology, cross to another location and then lure the beast into the portal. I knew that we had been stretching its capabilities when we made our hops to escape danger, but now, the massive bulk of the beast would probably cause the portal to melt down.

"So, having given you the coordinates, Melody and having instructed you to programme the beast to destroy what it saw at that location, I wanted to make sure it saw me. Hence why I was dancing in a rather strange fashion to attract its attention.

"It certainly worked, because once it had fixed its eyes on me, it knew that I was the target and it launched itself through the portal. At that point the technology failed. Half the Cryomorph was in the location I had just left and the other half was on my side of the portal. It was effectively sliced in two when the portal closed. If you were to peer through the airlock, you'd see half its remains lying on the floor in front of the wall."

"But where's the other half?" asked Xalata, "you must have only been in Habitat 14 all the time?"

"Correct, Xalata. I only made a small jump, just to a section of the habitat on the other side of the Control Room. Again, I wanted it to be on an outside wall with airlock protection in case my plan went wrong and the beast succeeded in passing through."

"But it didn't and you're here to tell the tale," said Melody.

"Yes, I am, but it's thanks to you two that we were able to do any of this. If you hadn't both tricked Fark, so that Brett floored him and so we got hold of the control for the Cryomorph, I dread to think what would have happened. His evil plan would have succeeded and we would have been left stuck on the Moon forever. More importantly, you've actually saved the Earth."

"Wow! Just like in the movies!" said Xalata and she and Melody burst out laughing.

*   *   *   *   *

The journey back to LunarBase was long and boring and the team all spent most of the time catching up on some much-needed sleep. Fark sat quietly, dozing, but it was evident that he had had the stuffing knocked out of him by the experience and, once he knew that Castrana had died in the attack by the Cryomorph, he became very subdued.

The train sped on and, later, it pulled into a makeshift station near to the main terminus at LunarBase. Everyone was dazed from sleep and boggled by their experiences so that, when they emerged into the main concourse and were met by a crowd of people, they were taken aback.

"Tell us what happened."

"How did you stop the asteroid?"

"Which one's Xalata and which one's Melody?"

The questions came thick and fast and Wiglet and Brett pushed a way through the jostling journalists and led the two girls and Glitch to the relative calm of a local food outlet. "I think before we do anything, we should eat - agreed?"

The two girls nodded enthusiastically and Glitch piped up, "Yeah, Mr O, I could eat a Cryomorph - fried perhaps?"

Melody and Xalata rolled their eyes at each other.

*   *   *   *   *

Back at the home, Melody and Xalata were greeted by a visibly relieved Dawn, who hugged her daughter hard and, with tears in her eyes, said to Brett, "Thank you so much, for bringing her ... them, both safe back. I can't thank you enough."

Brett smiled and looked at the two girls, "I think you'll find that it was more about them saving me than the other way round, actually." The girls laughed and Dawn smiled and then dashed over to give Brett a hug.

"I know I don't see you very often, even though we are next neighbours, but I would be devastated if anything happened to you. I'm so relieved to see you, all of you, back home safe and sound."

Brett put his arms around her and gave her a hug. "I think perhaps we need to make good on that and promise that we shall see each other from time to time."

The two girls looked at each other and both pulled a face, "Eugh!" said Xalata, "lovey-dovey talk! C'mon, Melody, you have practising to do." Xalata pulled her friend away from her mother and took her into the Fret's home. They closed the door. "I think it's best if we leave them to it, huh?" she said.

Melody nodded, with a grin. "OK - where's my gee-tar?" and she picked it up and started to play, really badly.

* * * * *

The next two days passed in a whirl. First up, they needed to watch the final moments of the asteroid as it plummeted towards Mars. Their programming had been spot on and the Mission Control in Beijing had now established a connection to control the project once more. Gathered together in Wiglet's home, the little group watched the readout from the cameras on board the asteroid and also from the impact site on Mars. It was only when they saw the bizarre images of a huge rock hurtling towards the surface of the planet that they realised how enormous it actually was. The size of a city block, it grew massively as the impact drew nearer until, all at once, it was upon the planet and all readout from those cameras ceased.

Satellite cameras took over and the view from space onto the surface of Mars showed an enormous plume of dust, rock and debris, ejected kilometres into the sky, leaving a mushroom cloud, not unlike the scene of an atomic explosion. Reports from the other side of the planet, where hardy pioneers were creating habitats, spoke of earthquakes and, after, a darkening of the sky as the dust circulated in the Martian atmosphere.

It would be many years before the true benefits of the impact would be revealed and there were to be other impacts in the future, all designed to help along the process of terraforming. But back on the Moon, there were scenes of jubilation from the group of heroes who had prevented the destruction of Earth.

Meanwhile, Adolf Fark had been taken to secure quarters where he was held under house arrest, pending a transfer to Earth and then a wait while evidence was gathered and a trial was put in place. The remains of Castrana Machin would be retrieved in due course and, now that the engineers had established that there was a viable route through the redundant tunnel around the Moon, teams of people would be sent out to retrieve the wreckage of Habitat 14 and to arrest Fark's henchmen.

*   *   *   *   *

There was much talking to be done, reports to be submitted and interviews to be had. The girls and Glitch were exhausted by the experience so that when, on the next day, they turned up at the Academy, they were unprepared for the welcome they received.

A throng of students met them as they walked into the large seminar room and everyone talked at once, wanting to know the full story. However, not everyone was so enthusiastic. "So, you saved the world and made it back, eh?" sneered Rose Pretty while Penny Wrath scowled from behind Rose's back. "Heroes in the classroom, my we are honoured! However, let's not forget that you are both fugitives and I should now be able to claim my reward. Something to do with illegal access to secure systems, if I remember correctly?" and she made a grab at her as if to restrain her.

Xalata stepped back and brushed away her hand, "Leave it Rose," she said with a tired voice.

"Or what?" said Rose aggressively. "Strikes me that you just skipped classes to go on a trip with your simpering little friend here. Big deal."

As Rose sauntered off to the other side of the room, Xalata turned away and Melody looked anxious. "Right," said Xalata to her friend, "You faced down the Cryomorph, rescued me and generally were a superhero ... and you're still afraid of Rose and Penny? C'mon, get serious!"

Melody looked at Xalata, "It's just that somehow, they're real and here and in my face where the Cryomorph and all that was just a dream that happened and anyone can be brave in dreams."

"You know what they say, Melody? Live the dream!"

Epilogue

Lessons at the Academy settled down into a more normal pattern. The girls studied hard, took exams, presented their findings and did well.

Melody entered Lunar Tunes with newfound confidence. She had followed Xalata's advice from what seemed ages before, had concentrated on learning the guitar piece and then had added the vocals. The result was good, but not good enough. She had dropped out of the contest in the first round and, although she was disappointed, she realised that she just couldn't do everything: studies, exams, Lunar Tunes, saving the world.

Xalata buried herself in her work, trying to forget the awful outcomes of her actions, but realising that they were more the fault of the people who started them than they were hers. As a result of the adventure they had been through together, she and Brett became closer and spent a great deal of time, discussing the past, looking to the future and working on scientific projects together. Brett and Dawn too, started to see more of each other, much to the two girls' amusement and delight.

The final exam season was coming for their year grade and so everyone was busy at their studies, both in the Academy and at home. On one particular day, Xalata had come into the seminar room where everyone studied during the week. No one else was in there except for her and Rose. They sat at opposite ends of the room and ignored each other until, after about an hour, Rose sauntered over to the table where Xalata sat.

"Xalata, my dear, dear friend," said Rose.

"Yeah, right," muttered Xalata.

"You and I have some talking to do."

"I don't think so."

"My friends and I don't like you."

"You have friends? Wow! Now that's an interesting snippet of news. Do they know?"

"Always ready with your sharp tongue, aren't you? Well, let's just say that my friends and I..."

"You mean Penny, I guess?"

"My friends and I have now lost patience with you."

"Meaning what?"

"Meaning..." Rose paused, "that we shall be waiting for you to fall and if we can help to give you a push, then we shall."

"You're weird. Leave me alone. I'll do the same."

Rose walked out of the room and Xalata sat there, fuming. Why should someone want to threaten her? What had Rose got against her? She was fed up with this psychological bullying and, at that moment, she jumped up and decided to do something about it. Dashing into the corridor she saw the door swing and Rose walking away from her into the atrium.

She was just about to follow her, when a voice stopped her. "So, Xalata, going somewhere in a hurry?" She turned and, to her horror, saw that it was Rose.

"But, you've..."

"What, Xalata? What is it? Lost your voice?" Rose sneered again and made to walk past her, but Xalata grabbed her arm.

"You just walked out that door," she said, "yet here you are. How can that be?"

"You're gibbering again. Mind's gone, blasted by monsters on Farside, I expect."

Xalata was certain of what she had seen and, without saying more, dashed out of Rose's presence and headed out to the atrium. *She can't have got far,* she thought as she searched, knowing that Rose would be heading for her home.

Then, in the distance, she caught sight of the tall figure of Rose, heading to the TransTrak and she dashed after her, pushing people out of the way in her certainty. As she arrived on the platform, the pod doors were just closing and she was too late. The TransTrak pulled out of the station and as the pods went past, Xalata's eyes met Rose's where she sat. There appeared to be two Rose Prettys.

The End

Now read the next thrilling story: *The Simulant Swarm* - the second book in the *Xalata Orbit and Melody Fret* series.

Simply visit the Amazon Kindle Book store and search "Xalata Orbit".

About the author

Nick Evans is a writer of non-fiction business and education books, so this first venture into fiction has been a bit traumatic. He started on the basis that he wanted to write dialogue - something he couldn't do - and now you'll know that he still can't do it!

He is a bit older than he'd like to be but younger than some people. He lives in Bournemouth in the UK and has no wish to go to the Moon. However, who knows what his grandkids might do?

He likes knowing what people think about his stuff, so if you fancy writing to him, just connect on nick@365notv.com - but be gentle. He's only human...

17501323R00134

Printed in Great Britain
by Amazon